A prisoner of fate, held captive by love

Alex leaned against the parapet of the castle's tower, bracing herself against the night wind as if challenging her very destiny.

But even the forces of nature could not sweep away her love for Philippe. It was as much a part of her as the child growing within her. Nothing could destroy that love. Not even the knowledge that Philippe would never love her as he loved his brother's wife....

Driven by her tortured emotions, Alex turned and ran recklessly down the twisting tower steps, suddenly crying out as she lost her footing. Her head struck stone, and then she plunged into the darkness....

Other titles by

CHARLOTTE LAMB
IN HARLEQUIN PRESENTS

Other titles by

CHARLOTTE LAMB
IN HARLEQUIN ROMANCES

Many of these titles, and other titles in the
Harlequin Romance series, are available at your
local bookseller or through the Harlequin Reader
Service. For a free catalogue listing all available
Harlequin Presents and Harlequin Romances,
send your name and address to:

HARLEQUIN READER SERVICE,
M.P.O. Box 707
Niagara Falls, N.Y. 14302

Canadian address:
Stratford, Ontario, Canada N5A 6W2
or use coupon at back of book.

CHARLOTTE LAMB

dark master

Harlequin Books

TORONTO • LONDON • NEW YORK • AMSTERDAM
SYDNEY • HAMBURG • PARIS

Harlequin Presents edition published August 1979
ISBN 0-373-70805-X

Original hardcover edition published in 1979
by Mills & Boon Limited

Printed in U.S.A.

CHAPTER ONE

ALEX ran lightly along the wooden groyne, her arms stretched out to their furthest length, balancing like an acrobat in the face of the strong westerly wind. Her green eyes laughed as she felt salt spray flung into her face. The waves crashed up on to the beach below, dragging back wet pebbles in a slow slide. Grey mists hung in impenetrable veils over the distant horizon. Occasionally a deep foghorn sounded within them like the wail of an animal in pain.

As a child Alex had spent hours balancing like this, hearing the mast wires of beached yachts jingling and the melancholy cry of yellow-beaked gulls overhead. There was a feeling of freedom, of risk, of excitement in what she was doing, pitting herself against the elements alone, always aware of the danger of falling, the wind tugging at her, making her jeans flap coldly against her calves and her long red-gold hair flare like a bright banner.

A wild, exultant feeling swept through her. She turned, laughter and recklessness in her face, to balance her way back to the beach.

It was at that instant that she saw the man standing watching her. She had thought herself totally alone in the early morning mist, and the surprise of his presence disturbed her. She halted suddenly and swayed. There was no time to regain her balance before she fell, but the stranger moved faster than she could think. She was received into hard, firm arms for a second before they both fell, rolling down the steeply shelving beach on sliding, wet pebbles.

'Oh, damn....' Alex muttered.

For a moment she lay, dazed, her head forced by a determined hand against his strong chest, hearing a strange, distant thunder which puzzled her until she realised it was the sound of his heart beneath her ear.

Pushing herself up, she looked down into a powerful, cold-featured face from which icy grey eyes surveyed her expressionlessly.

'I'm sorry,' she murmured, feeling colour rise in her cheeks.

'Did you hurt yourself?' he asked.

'No, thanks to you,' she said, offering him a polite little smile which received absolutely no response.

'You're lucky,' he retorted. 'A foolhardy game you were playing. You could so easily have fallen into the sea and drowned in this sort of weather.'

'That is very unlikely. I'm a very good swimmer and I'm used to walking along the groynes.'

'One should never underestimate the sea,' he said grimly.

He had, she realised, a faint accent. French? His English was excellent but slightly too good. She got up, brushing down her jeans. He rose, too, and she saw, with dismay, the salt stains on his obviously expensive dark grey suit.

'Oh, dear, I'm afraid your suit is ruined! You must allow me to pay to have it cleaned ...'

His dark brows rose and a look of hauteur crossed his face. 'I think not,' he drawled coldly.

'It was my fault,' she protested.

He did not dispute this, considering her, his mouth

wry. 'All the same, I will pay for my own cleaning bills,' he said.

'Well, thank you again, anyway,' she said hesitantly, beginning to back away.

'No more dangerous games,' he said, as if delivering an order.

Alex felt like curtseying. Did he know how he sounded? Or was he so used to giving commands that he no longer knew how to sound ordinarily human? A flicker of amusement crossed her face at the idea. There was so very little either ordinary or human about him. He was so tall and dominating in his formal clothes on this beach, a man out of his element, yet by sheer personality seeming to dwarf the wild power of sea and wind, as if he might, if he chose, force their capitulation, harness them to his will.

The grey eyes narrowed. 'Why the smile?' he asked, staring at her.

'I was thinking of King Canute,' she said on an impulse she should have checked.

A dark brow lifted. He turned his head, the wind lifting the thick black hair in a swathe, and stared across the misty water. 'Like him, I respect the sea,' he said. 'Only fools do not.'

'You're French?' she asked because that faint accent was tugging at her mind.

He looked back at her. 'Yes,' he agreed.

'On holiday?' she asked to make polite conversation.

'No,' he said, and the negative ended the exchange, making it plain to her that he disliked being asked questions.

She pushed back the windblown red-gold hair and gave him a cool, unsmiling nod. 'Well, thanks,' she said, and walked away up the beach without a backward glance.

She was on duty at nine. Slipping into the hotel through the staff entrance she went up to her room, showered, changed into the black dress she wore for work and went down to the staff dining-room to eat a light breakfast of toast and coffee.

Alex had been working at the Garth Hotel for a year. As the hotel receptionist her work was interesting and varied. She liked dealing with people. She had a warm, friendly nature as well as a calm refusal to fly into a panic which made her ideal for the job. She got on well with the other members of the staff, and the hotel manager, Hal Cecil, was her fiancé. It had been his idea that she should join the staff. It gave them a chance to see more of each other than might otherwise have been the case, since Hal's job kept him busy for most of the day. They had to snatch at opportunities to meet, and having Alex actually on the premises meant that Hal could always rely on seeing her if he could get away from his demanding role for half an hour. Even his evenings were often eaten into by guests who took it for granted that a hotel manager should always be available for consultation, complaint or courtesy whenever they wished to expect it.

The mist cleared gradually during the morning, and by noon the beach was crowded with holidaymakers lounging in the warm late summer sunshine. The wind had dropped. The sky was blue if a little troubled by fluffy white clouds, and the sea had calmed to a tranquil swell.

Hearing Hal's voice on the stairs, Alex glanced round and saw his fair head bent solicitously towards the elegant coiffure of one of their guests, a slim widow from Durham in a pale coffee linen dress of a very sophisticated yet simple cut, her brown curls clustered around a heart-shaped face which carried the mark of childlike sweetness and an incredible fragility. Deirdre Weatherby had been staying at the hotel for the past week, attracting both male and female eyes whenever she appeared. She was, Alex thought, watching her, extremely likeable, and that vulnerability of hers awoke sympathy on sight. Her husband of six months had been killed in a car crash a year ago, she had confided one morning, and this was her first holiday alone. She hated to be alone, she had sighed. The great brown eyes had looked at Alex appealingly. 'I get so frightened,' she had whispered. Alex had been touched, both by the confession and by the look of youth about her, although Deirdre was, in fact, a year older than herself. Somehow her five foot three and her petite delicacy made her look at least two years younger. Alex had felt much older, stronger, more resilient as she watched Deirdre sigh.

She watched now, seeing Hal's attractive blue eyes soften as the other girl sighed up at him. Hal was sorry for Deirdre, too, she thought with warmth. He was a kind man and he must find it as touching as she did to watch Deirdre attempting to face her empty future bravely.

Sensing herself under surveillance she turned quickly, adopting a polite smile, and felt her smile freeze under the impact of cold grey eyes.

For a moment she was too taken aback to speak. Then she pulled herself together and said courteously, 'Good morning. Can I help you?'

'My key,' he said in a clipped tone. 'Room 3.'

She was surprised. She had never seen him here

before. Room 3 had been vacated the previous day, however, so she imagined he must have arrived last night after she went off duty. Turning, she reached down the key and handed it to him. 'Here you are, sir,' she said politely.

Just for an instant she imagined that he must have failed to recognise her. On the beach this morning in her old, crumpled jeans and thin sweater, her hair loose, she must have been a different person from the cool, formally clad receptionist facing him now. He swung the key on his finger, looking her up and down with a bland lack of expression which concealed his thoughts. 'No ill effects from your stumble this morning?' he enquired, making it clear he did recognise her.

Her face was as blank as his own. 'No, thank you, sir,' she said in cold tones.

He nodded and turned away to the lift. When he had gone she looked at the register and read his name. Philippe de Villone. The name of his home was unfamiliar to her. Sarconne. A French town? Or village? She looked at the black, powerful handwriting. It would have told her a good deal about him even if she had never set eyes on him.

She had her lunch and returned to the desk at two. The afternoon was busy and she only saw Hal briefly. They smiled at each other once or twice as he passed, but he was engrossed in his job and had no time today to stand and talk. At six the evening relief arrived, a friendly local girl who was married with a small child and worked part-time to help the family budget. She worked until ten when the night porter took over. Alex chatted to her for a few moments, waiting for Hal, who usually joined her to arrange what they should do in the evening if he could get some free time. She sauntered across to the stairs, intending to go up to Hal's office, as he had not arrived, and walked straight into Philippe de Villone. She stood back, a cool smile on her face, waiting for him to pass her. Instead he stopped and surveyed her with that unsmiling grey glance.

'As you are a guest, m'sieur,' she said, uneasy under his stare, 'perhaps you would allow me to see to it that your grey suit is cleaned by our own staff ...'

'I've already seen to that,' he said calmly.

'Oh, good,' she stammered, wondering why he was staring at her so oddly.

'Since you mention it, however,' he went on quietly, 'you do owe me something, so perhaps you will have dinner with me tonight? I am alone in a strange town and I am bored.'

The request took her breath away. It was almost insulting in the way he phrased it. Her colour rose and her green eyes were barbed, as she retorted, 'What a very gracious invitation! Almost irresistible, m'sieur, but I'm afraid the staff are not encouraged to socialise with the guests. It sometimes gives male guests a false impression.'

His dark eyes lifted. 'I merely asked for your company at dinner, not in bed, mademoiselle.'

Her colour deepened. 'Well, that's a relief,' she snapped on impulse.

Hal's voice behind her made her turn her head. He was speaking to someone beside the lifts and moved towards her as he caught sight of her, a smile on his face. 'Darling, I'm sorry,' he said apologetically. 'I kept you waiting again. I got held up.' Then he glanced at the guest and gave a very polite smile. 'Good evening, m'sieur. I hope you are enjoying your stay with us.'

'Very much,' said Philippe de Villone, calmly study-ing Hal as if curious about him.

'Excellent,' Hal said warmly. He smiled at Alex. 'I'm afraid I have to finish a pile of paperwork. I won't be free until nine. Why not have dinner and wait for me?'

'Yes,' she smiled back, putting a hand on his arm in token of her understanding that he had no option but to consider his job first. She was used to coming second by now.

He leant forward and kissed her briefly. 'See you.' Giving a polite half bow to the other man, he vanished back towards the lifts and she turned to go upstairs, finding herself once more facing Philippe de Villone.

This time he took her left hand in his, holding the wrist so that he could inspect her diamond engagement ring. 'You are engaged,' he murmured flatly.

'Yes,' she said, resenting something in his derisive grey eyes.

'To the hotel manager? How romantic!'

His tone implied the opposite and she flushed.

'A recent betrothal?' he asked, raising his grey eyes to her flushed face.

'We've been engaged for a year,' she said between tight lips.

His brows rose almost into his dark hair. 'A year?' His mouth twisted. 'But then you live under the same roof ...'

Her eyes flashed. 'What's that supposed to imply?'

He shrugged, smiling satirically. 'What do you think? And why not? This is a permissive age.'

'For you, perhaps,' she said crisply. 'Not for me.'

'Poor fellow,' he murmured. 'No wonder he prefers to work late!'

Alex drew a sharp breath, then closed her lips on the angry words which sprang forward on her tongue. Her features froze. 'Excuse me,' she said, stepping round him and moving up the stairs. As she turned the corner on to the next landing she glanced back and saw him watching her from the bottom of the stairs, his hands in his pockets and a totally unreadable expression on his hard face.

Quickly she turned her head away and vanished out of his view. In her own room she drew the curtains and sat down on the bed, her face discontented. She had been looking forward to spending an evening with Hal. Lately he had been kept so busy that she had seen little of him. The summer season was difficult, of course. In the winter they managed to see far more of each other. Their wedding was planned for that winter, in fact, although no actual date had yet been decided upon. They would be free to take their honeymoon when Hal got a replacement from the London company who owned the hotel.

She sighed and got up. Slowly she changed out of her black uniform and took a long shower, feeling the tension of the day softly leave her tired muscles. Dressed in a vivid green dress, her red-gold hair piled on the back of her head, leaving her long neck bare, she went downstairs to dinner. For the evening meal it was accepted that staff might eat in the hotel dining-room, since only a few ate in the hotel at night. Most of the staff were local and went home in the evening.

As she entered the dining-room Philippe de Villone rose from his chair and indicated the place opposite him. Alex gave him a brief, cold look, pausing. 'No, thank you, m'sieur.'

Before he had time to respond she walked past him and went to the table in the corner, reserved for staff, joining several others who were eating there. They greeted her with friendly enthusiasm. She was well liked on the staff and had made a number of good friends in the town since her arrival.

Within a few moments she had forgotten Philippe de Villone and was laughing at an anecdote told by one of the floor maids, her green eyes bright with amusement.

Just as she was finishing her coffee, Hal said behind her, 'I'm sorry, darling. You can hit me if you like. I got behind with that stuff during the day and it has to go off first post tomorrow.'

She turned her red head to smile at him lovingly, and he bent and kissed her lightly on her cheek. 'You are the most forgiving girl.'

'Are you going to have dinner now?' she asked.

'I had something in my office on a tray,' he said. 'Shall we take a walk along the front? It is quite warm.'

'That would be nice,' she agreed, rising.

They walked out of the dining-room hand in hand, passing Philippe de Villone, whose cold grey eyes observed their linked hands and rose sardonically to meet Alex's glance. She icily met his look, then glanced away. He was an insufferable man, she thought, and almost told Hal what he had said, only to think better of it, because Hal would undoubtedly warn her not to say anything to the brute which could be interpreted as discourtesy. The worst sin a member of the staff could commit was to be rude to a guest, and she could well imagine Philippe de Villone taunting her into making a sharp remark, then complaining of it to the management.

They walked along the front, watching the silver path the moon had laid out across the sea, stretching far out to the horizon over the clear calm waters as far as the eye could see. There was no hint of mist tonight. The sky was a deep, unclouded mirror above the moonlit sea and the waves whispered gently as they slid up on to the beach.

Alex leaned her head upon Hal's shoulder as they paused to stare out to sea. 'The season will be over before we know where we are, and then we can start planning our wedding,' she murmured.

'Yes,' he said flatly.

She looked up at his rugged profile, frowning. 'Is something wrong? You sound angry.'

'Just staff trouble,' he said. 'Forget it. I don't want to bring my work out here with me.' He turned and put his arms around her waist, bending his head, and Alex raised her mouth eagerly for his kiss.

'Hal, darling,' she whispered as their mouths met, her arms twining round his neck.

Then a sound split them apart and they both turned, surprised, to see Philippe de Villone just behind them, sauntering along, his hands in his pockets, a mocking tilt to his dark head. Flushed, Hal took Alex's arm and began to walk back towards the hotel rapidly. She felt a bitter anger against the Frenchman for having interrupted a precious moment. She and Hal were so rarely alone. Lately she had begun to feel completely frustrated, never able to spend more than a few moments with him each day. It was maddening to have had this

time cut short. As she passed him, she gave the Frenchman a cold glare of hatred which she did not bother to
disguise.

Over the next few days she was kept as busy as usual,
seeing Hal rarely and only for a short time, and, she
was grateful to find, seeing little of Philippe de Villone
either. He was in England on business, she discovered,
and one evening he held a dinner party at the hotel,
ordering a very special meal for his guests, six of them
sharing a table set apart from the other guests, attracting all eyes by their air of exclusiveness and quite obvious wealth. The three women were all so exquisitely
gowned, so well groomed from head to toe, sweeping
into the hotel with an air of condescension which Alex
found irritating. Their escorts were from the same box,
she told herself, watching them later as they all moved
away from their table, smoking cigars, laughing, a flush
of good wine and talk on their faces. Except Philippe
de Villone, of course ... there was no flush on his face,
no relaxed smile on his face. He looked, as always, cold,
sardonic, aware.

When his guests had gone he came back into the
hotel just as she was walking up the stairs towards her
own room. She turned her head slightly as he appeared
beside her, feeling an odd contraction somewhere inside her, as if some internal muscle had jerked at the
sight of him.

The grey eyes glinted down at her. 'No moonlight
strolls tonight?' he asked drily.

'No,' she said shortly. Hal had been too busy all
evening to come down and talk to her.

'Too bad,' he said.

They turned the corner on to the first floor and she
was about to walk away from him to the small stair

which led to the staff rooms, when the door of Deirdre Weatherby's room opened and both she and Philippe de Villone saw Hal, his arms around the other girl's slim body, kissing her with passion. Alex froze, pain and incredulity in her face. Without even knowing it, she closed a hand on Philippe de Villone's arm, her fingers biting into his flesh to help her to contain the cry of anguish which was rising to her lips.

'I can't hurt her, darling,' Hal whispered, so audibly it made Alex's blood chill in her veins. 'I just can't bring myself to tell her.'

'I must go away,' Deirdre said, a sob in her voice. 'It's wrong. I must go tomorrow, Hal.'

Philippe de Villone acted so fast Alex had no time to work out what he was doing. One moment she was riveted to the spot, her eyes on the couple framed in the doorway. The next she was in the linen room in the dark, a hand over her mouth, with no idea how she had come there.

She stared up over the hand, mumbling angrily against it.

'Ssh!' he hissed.

They both heard the closing of a door along the corridor. Then footsteps, the whirr of the lift, the lift door open and close. Silence descended.

The hand moved away from her mouth. Philippe de Villone opened the door and peered out, then pulled her out after him. She was shivering, in a state of shock, as yet mindlessly unable to think about what she had seen and heard. She leaned against the wall, her eyes shut, trying to cope with the sickness in the pit of her stomach. She felt her arm taken and was pulled forward.

Opening her eyes, she found herself being propelled

into his room and halted, digging in her heels like a recalcitrant mule. 'No.'

He turned a brilliant grey glance down on her face. 'Don't be a little fool!'

The scathing note in the voice got through to her. She allowed him to push her down into a chair and sat, her hands on her lap, faintly quivering. He closed the door and moved quietly around the room. After a moment he bent over her, putting a glass into her hand. She looked at it numbly. 'No, thanks.'

'Drink it,' he said curtly. 'You need it.'

When she made no move to obey, his hand lifted it to her mouth and with a faint sigh she drank some, coughing as the heat of the spirit reached her throat.

He leaned against the dressing-table, his arms folded, staring at her. 'So you had no idea,' he drawled.

Alex looked at him in bewilderment. 'What?'

His mouth compressed. 'Even I knew,' he said tersely.

She stared, a flush rising in her face. 'You knew ... what?'

'My God, haven't you any eyes? The first time I saw them together I knew. He fell like a ton of bricks ... the sweet, helpless little widow gave him one look and he was finished. I thought one of your friends would have enlightened you. Your fiancé has been seeing her every evening this week while you've been hanging around waiting for him.' His voice had a sardonic note which increased her humiliated flush.

She had had no idea, no suspicion, but now she looked back over the past ten days and had a hundred pictures flashing through her mind ... Hal avoiding her, Hal seen at a distance with Deirdre, his head protectively bent over her, his blue eyes following her as she walked away ... She had thought his kindness, his attention, was due to pity. Then she remembered odd silences when she joined a group of the staff, little glances, sudden cessation of talk.

They had all guessed, all suspected, except herself. She was sick with humiliation and wounded pride. They must have been talking and laughing behind her back, amused by her total blindness. That Hal could have done this to her ... She was shattered.

'I trusted him,' she said, to herself, yet aloud.

'What are you going to do?' Philippe de Villone asked, watching her white face closely.

She lifted the green eyes to his hard features almost helplessly, as if asking him to tell her. 'I don't know.'

His brows drew together. 'You can't just ignore it. I thought it was just a passing affaire. I thought that was what you were doing ... ignoring it.' He shrugged cynically. 'After all, in the hotel game I suppose these things do happen all the time. For all I knew he was always flirting with female guests. But from what we overheard tonight I suspect there was more to it than that ... it sounded real.'

She shuddered. It had sounded very real to her, too. Deirdre had sounded heartbroken, Hal had sounded desperate, and she thought of his odd behaviour recently, odd gaps in their conversation, strange uncertain looks. Had he been trying to get the courage to speak to her about it?

She got up and walked angrily to the window, pulling the curtain aside to stare down at the moonlit sea. 'Oh, damn!' she muttered. 'I shall have to ... what? Ask him?' Her colour rose again and she turned and looked at him. 'What do I say? Excuse me, Hal, I know we're engaged, but are you in love with another woman?' Her voice was brittle. 'We've been engaged for a year. I thought I knew him, but now I find I didn't know him at all.'

'He fell in love with someone else. I doubt if it was something he wanted to happen,' said the cold voice. 'You just have to face it.'

'I have,' she said tightly. 'I am. That doesn't solve the problem of what the hell I'm going to do.'

His mouth tightened. 'Simple, isn't it? Break your engagement.'

'Just walk up to him and say: sorry, it's all off? Without a reason?' Her green eyes flashed. 'If I'd found out he was cheating me all the time it would be different. Then I could hate him and forget it. But it isn't his fault, is it? As you said, he just fell out of love with me and into love with her ... so, without making things worse, how do I tell him I know and it doesn't matter?'

'Is that what you want?' he asked oddly. 'To free him without making waves?'

Her chin lifted and a proud, angry look came into the green eyes. 'Just that. Whatever I do, whatever I say, though, he's bound to know I blame him. It will leave a stain, won't it? Guilt always does.'

'You must give him a good reason, then,' he said coolly. 'One which will seem to have nothing to do with him.'

Alex listened hopefully. 'Such as? That I found I've fallen out of love with him suddenly?' Her mouth shook. 'He won't believe that.' The green eyes were filled with sadness. 'I don't think I could make it convincing enough.'

'That you find you've fallen for someone else,' he said flatly.

She laughed wildly. 'Oh, great. Who? The night

porter? Don't be stupid, Monsieur de Villone ... Hal knows I haven't met anyone else.'

'You've met me,' he said drily.

She did not take it in for a moment, her face irritated. 'There hasn't been an opportunity for me to meet anyone.' Then her voice died away and she looked at him in astonishment, flushing.

'I will make it extremely convincing,' he said, his French accent stronger than usual. He picked up the telephone and rang down to the desk, asking for a bottle of champagne to be sent to his room. Alex was struck dumb, staring at him, her brows knit.

'What are you talking about?' she asked. 'I don't understand.'

He took her arm and pushed her towards the bathroom. She resisted, her eyes on his face. 'What are you doing? What's going on?'

He bent down, saying, 'Kick off your shoes.'

'What?' Distraught, she tried to push him away, but he lifted one foot and quickly threw her shoe into a corner of the room. 'Stop that!' she exclaimed, wondering if he was insane. The other shoe was gone, lying half under the bed, then he pushed her into the bathroom, saying, 'Be quiet and stay there until I call you.'

She backed and sat on the edge of the bath, wondering if she had lost possession of her senses. She heard the door open, heard the floor waiter's voice, the click of glasses, the sudden explosion of the cork. Then the door closed and the French voice called softly, 'You can come out now.'

Alex went out, her face curious, and halted, staring in disbelief. He was lying on the crumpled bed, his tie gone, his shirt open, his jacket discarded.

Flushing deeply, she edged round the room towards

the door, furious at her own stupidity.

'Where do you think you're going?' he asked her, amusement in his voice.

'To my own room,' she said tightly. 'If you think I'm going to stay here all night you can think again. I might have known you were an opportunist!'

He laughed. 'How like a woman, suspicious where there's no cause, blind in the face of all the evidence ... sit down, you silly girl. This is the convincing evidence for your fiancé, don't you see? The floor waiter is not blind. He saw your shoes, and recognised them.' He leant over, his long lean body graceful, and picked the shoe up from beneath the bed, holding it out to her. 'Very pretty shoes, too ... distinctive ... that green is unusual. Oh, yes, the floor waiter knew whose shoes they were.'

She stared, taking it in at last, scarlet sweeping up to her hair. 'You wanted him to ... oh, my God, my reputation will be nil by tomorrow! Is that your idea of helping me?'

'You lost your head,' he drawled lazily. 'My persuasion was quite irresistible and you love me.'

'Oh, shut up!' she muttered, her hands clenched. But it was one way out, that was true. She could go to Hal and tell him she had fallen madly in love, lost her head. The staff gossip would convince him of the truth and he need not feel so badly about breaking the engagement. 'Of course, he'll be shocked,' she thought aloud, shamed humiliation in her face. To save Hal's face must she lose her own self-respect like this? 'Why didn't you tell me what you meant to do?' she asked him furiously. 'It makes me look ...' She broke off, biting her lip. 'Did the whole hotel have to hear about it? In twenty-four hours all my friends will know that

I was in here with you. It would be bad enough to let
Hal think such things of me, but to have the whole
world knowing is damnable!'

'What difference does it make?' he drawled, watching her. 'You'll be leaving here anyway.'

For a few seconds Alex merely stared at him in con-
sternation, then she saw the cold common sense of what
he had said. Of course she would have to leave. She
could not stay here after this—she had to put distance
between herself and Hal. She had to extricate herself
from the humiliating muddle of her life.

He poured a glass of champagne, offered it to her.
'Relax,' he drawled. 'There's something I want you
to do for me.'

She sipped the pale golden liquid, considering him.
'Anything I can do, of course,' she said soberly. 'You've
been very kind. I may regret your method of breaking
my engagement, but I can see it will seem very convincing to Hal. I'm in no mood to discuss things with
him, anyway. I would prefer to end it quickly.' She
grimaced. 'I shall go back to London and get a job
there. I worked there happily before I met Hal. I'm
sure I can get a reference from a friend of mine without Hal finding out.'

'There's no need for that,' he said, refilling her glass.

She laughed. 'Of course there is—I need a job with a
room thrown in, I hate living in bedsitting-rooms
alone. Hotel life is what I'm used to now.' She contem-
plated her glass, sipping at it slowly and pleasurably.
The champagne was making her head seem very clear
and alive. 'I've no family, you see. My parents died
when I was fifteen.' She grimaced. 'Lucky now—there's
nobody to ask awkward questions. I lived with foster-
parents until I was seventeen, but we never got on

well. As soon as I was old enough to leave I got a job in a London hotel, and I've been working in hotels ever since. That's how I met Hal.' Her eyes darkened as she remembered the heady joy of falling in love and being loved in return. It had been so new to her, that shared delight. Now she saw it had been an illusion.

Leaning forward, he poured a little more champagne into her empty glass and she lifted it almost gratefully to her lips. It was making the sick whirl of her misery recede a little. It was also, she thought with amusement, making her talkative, but Philippe seemed interested in what she was saying, so that did not matter.

'Hal was working at the same London hotel,' she said slowly. 'When he got this job he persuaded me to come down and work here, so that we could be together. It was odd, because I used to stay here as a child for summer holidays, and I loved the place. I was so happy to be coming here to live ...' Breaking off, on the point of tears, she said huskily, 'You said you wanted to ask a favour? What was it, m'sieur?'

'You speak French, don't you?' he asked, his grey eyes level on her face.

She nodded. 'It helps to have languages in the hotel trade.'

'You need to get away from here,' he said, as if talking through a train of thought which had sprung to his mind. 'I need your help.'

Hazily she regarded him with a frown. 'What sort of help?'

'I want you to marry me,' he said.

For a moment she thought her ears were playing tricks. She stared blankly at him. The hard face was expressionless, the grey eyes watchful. She laughed lightly. 'I thought you said ...'

'I did say it,' he said drily. 'I have a good reason.'

Alex wondered if the champagne was affecting her mind more strongly than she had suspected. 'What sort of reason?' she asked, frowning, trying to concentrate.

'The same sort as your own,' he said. 'The woman I love prefers another man, and I want to prove to her that I don't give a damn.'

She felt a surge of fellow feeling. Gazing at him through the golden haze the champagne had engendered, she said mildly, 'It's damnable, isn't it? To be in love with someone who doesn't feel the same way. One doesn't want anyone to guess, let alone them.' His confession had softened her view of him. She had never suspected that a man of his self-confidence and attraction could harbour such feelings, but eyeing the powerful profile and hard, sensual mouth, she guessed suddenly, with a curious little shiver, that he was a man capable of violent, dangerous emotions but capable, too, of suppressing and disguising them at the command of that cold brain of his.

'Wounded animals always hide,' he shrugged. 'The deepest thickets provide the best cover. Will you marry me and help me to disguise how I feel? We can be of use to each other. You need to get away from here. I need your help.'

She found it hard to concentrate. Her thoughts dissolved in a bright mist as if they were champagne bubbles. 'It's absurd,' she said with slurred emphasis.

'It would be very convincing, though,' he said softly. 'It is too final to be a pretence.'

'I never heard such a ridiculous idea,' she said, staring at him, her green eyes over-bright.

'I'm offering you escape and a salve for your pride,' he said. 'I need your help as much as you needed mine.

remember. In any case, you're committed now to either appearing to be my mistress or my wife. Would you rather that Hal thought you capable of going to bed at the drop of a hat or believed you were swept off your feet by love?'

She took it in slowly. Her brain was working well below par. 'That's blackmail!'

He shrugged. 'I need your help badly and I don't care how I get it.'

'You expect a lot in return for what you've done for me,' she said angrily.

'That's the way I am.'

'Yes,' she said, staring at him. She remembered him suddenly on the beach the first time they had met, defying the wind and waves with those cold grey eyes, like King Canute, and could imagine that he did, indeed, impose his personality on everyone he met. A strong, tough, ruthless man who went straight for what he wanted without caring who or what got in the way.

'I don't,' she said slowly, 'like you very much.'

He took away her empty glass. 'You've had enough of that,' he drawled wryly.

'It isn't just the champagne talking,' she told him clearly. 'I don't trust you.'

He looked down into her flushed, drowsy face, his own eyes quite brilliant and filled with amusement. 'You can trust me, Alex,' he told her tolerantly.

His hard profile seemed to be wavering as though under water, and she half closed her eyes to keep it in perspective.

He bent down, sliding an arm around her, and she protested, her hands pushing at his chest.

'What are you doing?' she asked, a frown on her face.

'You're under the weather,' he said with a smile in

his voice. 'Relax, *chérie*. You're in no danger from me.'

Alex leaned against him, thinking how effortlessly he carried her across the room, how strong the arm beneath her languid body felt. His dark face was close to hers and she considered it through her half-closed lids, thinking of his wild suggestion earlier.

'Nobody gets married for such a silly reason,' she muttered, half to herself.

'People do stranger things for the sake of their pride,' he told her without emphasis.

Her head went round as he lowered her. She tried to wake up, feeling the bed softly giving beneath her body, but it was just too difficult to prise her lids open. Someone detached her arms from their clutch around some warm, hard neck. She muttered drowsily, turning on to her side. The warm haze of the champagne was like a pleasant sea on which she floated. She felt the gentle brush of hands upon her body, firm, authoritative and deft. No alarm bells rang in her head. Sleep held her in its toils and she made no effort to surface from it.

Somewhere at a distance she began to hear Hal's voice. It sounded sharp and incredulous. She turned on her side, burrowing a hand under her long, loose hair, her body sliding beneath the sheet, then felt herself coming slowly back to the surface of consciousness as she grew more alert and aware. Her lids flickered open. The room was full of daylight. And voices—angry voices.

She stared across at Hal's flushed, bitter face, sat up instinctively, then with a muffled squeak of astonishment and shock flew back underneath the sheet as she realised she was only wearing her underclothes.

'My God!' Hal exclaimed furiously. 'I'd never have

believed it of you, Alex, if I hadn't seen it with my
own eyes!' His blue gaze was filled with distaste and
her cheeks burned beneath that look, shame and remorse in her lowered eyes.

'I'm sorry, Hal,' she whispered, feeling as guilty as
if she had done what he obviously thought she had.
'I'm terribly sorry.'

'It just happened,' Philippe de Villone said flatly.
He came over to the bed, sat down beside her, wearing
a silk dressing-gown beneath which it was pretty plain,
even to her gaze, that he wore absolutely nothing at
all. 'Can't you understand love striking like that? A
look? A terrible urgency? Come on, man, we understand how badly you must feel, but you have to be able
to understand us.'

'Love?' Hal's voice spat out the word. 'Is that how
you describe it?'

'I want to marry her,' Philippe said curtly. 'I will
marry her. That is why I brought you here ... to hear
the truth. We love each other. We don't want to hurt
you, but we want to get married right away.'

There was a silence. Alex looked at Hal beneath
her lashes unhappily. He was staring at her. Philippe
put an arm around her, holding her against him so that
she felt the hard warmth of his body striking through
the silk of his dressing-gown. Weakly she leaned her
head against him, grateful for the physical support.

'Well, there is nothing I can say, is there?' said Hal.
'Except good luck.' The distaste and anger had gone
out of his face and he looked oddly tired, his mouth
grim.

Philippe held out his hand. 'There's this,' he said.

Only then did Alex see her engagement ring had
gone from her hand. It lay in Philippe's palm, spark-

ling in the sunlight. Hal stared at it.

'Keep it,' he said curtly, turning on his heel. The door banged behind him, and Alex gave a low cry of pain.

'How could you?' She turned on Philippe bitterly. 'Why did you bring him in here, make him think I would do a thing like that? Why did you have to interfere? I must have been mistaken. He looked so hurt, so shocked ... there must be some other explanation. He couldn't have been in love with her after all.'

'Of course not,' said Philippe, his mouth wry. 'Did you think she was the first? Your friends on the staff have been too kind, too discreet all along ... don't you see that now? He is a flirt. He never goes too far, just a pleasant little game with the unattached female guests, with the ones who won't make waves for him with you. Then when they have gone home there you are ... sweet, loyal, unsuspicious Alex, waiting for him. Like a sailor, he likes variety but a good wife in the background too.'

'You're lying,' she said. 'Hal wouldn't ... I must have been mad to listen to you from the start!' She thought of Hal, kind, loving, reliable. She had known him for eighteen months. They had been engaged for a year. How could she have believed him to be unfaithful to her on such flimsy evidence? And then listen to this man, whom she did not even know, a stranger with a face like granite and a cold, hard manner, telling her that Hal, of all people, was a flirt and had been deceiving her for months. 'I don't believe it!'

'Ask your friends,' he shrugged. 'Of course they have kept it quiet from you. They were sorry for you. You are well liked among the staff, I gather, but my chambermaid was quite forthcoming to me, a guest who seemed to know some of the gossip already ... she sat in this room and told me a good deal about you and your handsome fiancé, who was known to them all as a flirt.' He grimaced. 'Oh, never with anyone on the staff—he has too much good sense for that. He picks his victims carefully. Lonely, attractive women who will be grateful for little attentions. A few kisses, compliments, sighs ... I do not even imagine he always sleeps with them.'

'Oh!' Alex covered her face with her hands. 'It isn't true!'

'I think you are beginning to believe it,' he said flatly. 'And you can soon find out—ask your friends ... go on, get dressed and go and ask them now. Tell them your engagement is over and listen while it all pours out, as it will once they are sure you will not be hurt by the truth.'

'Why didn't someone tell me?' she groaned.

'They wanted to be kind. Instead they were cruel,' he said.

'But why should he?' she asked wildly. 'Why?'

He shrugged. 'It pleases him, satisfies his vanity. If you had married him it would have gone on throughout your married life and he would have made you very unhappy. Some men cannot live without a changing supply of female admiration, and he is one.' He moved to the door. 'Get dressed, go to your room and pack. We are leaving.'

'Now?' She looked lost. Her world had been turned upside down in a few hours and she did not know what to do.

'We are going to London to get married,' he explained. 'It will be easier to do it quickly there.'

'I just can't walk out like this!'

'You can and will,' he said flatly.

'My job ...'

'Someone else will do it. Nobody is irreplaceable, remember that. We leave in an hour.'

He was gone before Alex had a chance to say anything. She slowly got out of the bed and began to get washed and dressed. She did not even notice the tears which were pouring down her face. Someone else walked out of that room, went to her bedroom and packed all her things. Someone else walked down to reception, carrying her case. Janet Day was on the desk, flicking over the letters. She looked up and stared curiously, eyes wide, as Alex approached. Alex saw that the gossip was all round the hotel. Flushed, bright-eyed, from tears, not joy, she said, 'Goodbye, Janet.'

'You're going?' Janet whispered. 'Hal said you were, but I ...'

'What did Hal say?' Alex asked. 'That we were no longer getting married? It's true.'

'I suppose you found out?' Janet said sadly, a kind, brown-eyed girl with a thin face and a gentle smile. 'I'm so sorry, Alex. We never liked to say anything, because it never seemed to mean anything to him. He just likes to chat up other women, I suppose, and they come and go ... you seemed happy enough, so we let well alone.'

Alex preserved a smile by sheer effort of will power. 'That's in the past,' she said flatly.

Then Philippe was there, taking her case and her arm, his grip possessive. 'Ready, *chérie*?' he asked with tender accents which made Janet's eyes widen.

'Yes,' said Alex, 'I'm ready, Philippe.'

He helped her into his car and took the seat behind the wheel, glancing at her. 'Did I gather you had had confirmation?' he asked quietly.

'As if you didn't know,' she said bitterly. 'I must be deaf, dumb and blind, it seems ... all these months, a conspiracy to keep me ignorant. God, I feel such a damned fool!'

'How old are you?' he asked, his face gentle. 'Twenty-one? Two?'

'Twenty-two,' she admitted.

'I am senior by twelve years,' he said. 'Thirty-four. So I have some right to give you advice. We learn only by experience, Alex. Advice alone is never enough. You would have found out one day. You are lucky to find out before you married him ... your life would have been hell if you had been his wife.'

She nodded. Then, pain in her voice, she said, 'I could have sworn he loved me.'

Philippe started the car. 'Perhaps he did, in his way. Is that love what you wanted, a love you had to share with every attractive woman ready to encourage him?'

She shivered. 'No. Oh, no!'

Philippe looked sideways grimly. 'Nor me, *chérie*. My woman would be mine and no other man's ever. I never share, most of all not a woman.'

'Was your girl-friend unfaithful?' she asked him curiously, seeing the brilliant gleam of his grey eyes.

'She was never mine,' he said curtly.

'You just wanted her to be?'

He nodded. 'But she chose someone else. So.' He shrugged. 'We have nothing but our pride, do we?'

Alex shivered, this time quite violently. 'A cold thought.' She looked out of the window. 'Where are we going?'

'London,' he said. 'To be married.'

'You're not serious,' she said weakly. 'You can't mean

it. We know nothing about each other. It's lunacy!'

'Common sense,' he said. 'I need a wife, you need to get away. You will like my home; it is very beautiful.'

'Sarconne,' she said, remembering the name in the register. 'Is that a town?'

Philippe laughed. 'A town? No, no. Sarconne is ...' He paused, a look of amusement on his face. 'You will see what Sarconne is as soon as we are within sight of it.'

CHAPTER TWO

ALEX understood ten days later when they drove through Limousin, in the warm fertile south of France. She first saw Sarconne in the distance, its conical towers piercing the surrounding woods and reaching up to the brilliant blue sky. She felt Philippe's glance slip over her face and turned to smile at him. 'A castle!' she exclaimed, as yet not realising. 'Like something out of a fairy story ... isn't it lovely? But then all of this is so lovely. I had no idea France was so beautiful.' The landscape was strikingly dramatic, changing suddenly from deep, fertile valleys dreaming in the summer sunlight to great swelling hillsides which had been densely cultivated over the centuries, their slopes rich with vines. The roads were narrow and wound from valley to hill in a serpentine fashion, twisting to give sudden insights into the nature of the countryside; deeply wooded, silvered with wandering streams, enriched by tall, green-leaved maize, rolling smoothly around the small towns.

It was three days since they had married in London. Alex had lost none of her anxious doubts about the wisdom of what she was doing, but Philippe would not permit her to reconsider, sweeping her along on a ceaseless course of action which left her no time to sit down and think straight. There had been so many things to do; her passport had been dealt with, her trousseau bought, the details of their wedding arranged. She had felt like a straw on flood water as he rushed her from place to place. He had not left her alone during the day. When they were not organising their marriage, he took her around London on a sightseeing tour, making her act as his guide to the beauty spots of the capital, although she strongly suspected he knew the city almost as well as she did. In the evenings they dined together, quite late, so that by the time they parted she was tired and able to sleep deeply, her mind dazed by the excellent wine he always ordered with the meal. At times she awoke early in the morning and felt panic and dismay creeping into her mind as she realised what was happening to her. Philippe had taken over her life. He was manipulating her, as if he were a puppetmaster and she a wooden doll. His ruthless insistence on his own way alarmed and angered her, but these moments of panic always dissolved once she was in his presence again, as if the hypnotic glance of those grey eyes could control even her secret thoughts.

She knew no more about him now than she had the first day they met. He refused to talk about his home, saying she would soon see it for herself. He told her little about his family, his tone guarded. She knew that he was involved in the wine trade—that much he had indicated. She knew that he liked paintings—he made a point of visiting several London art galleries. She knew he liked music—he took her twice to concerts, and from what he said she had discovered something of his musical taste, enough to know he had a particular partiality for the violin, and loved Debussy's music, had, he said, a wide collection of French music on record. She had smiled teasingly. 'Chauvinist!'

'All Frenchmen are,' he said drily, but he smiled back.

Oddly, he knew far more about her than she did

about him. He asked her many questions about herself, very casually, throwing them out in conversation so lightly that she barely noticed how much she was telling him about her life until it dawned on her one day that her whole life was an open book to him. He had a retentive, shrewd intelligence which absorbed and held everything she said to him, she soon found, and she began to resent the fact that she should be so unenlightened about him while he should know so much about her.

Wryly, she stared ahead at the countryside through which they were driving. There was so little to tell him about herself, to tell the truth. She had no past, no family, no home ... a rootless creature without any interest for someone as hard and self-assured as Philippe de Villone. Despite her brilliant red-gold hair and green eyes, she was colourless and dull—a sheet of paper on which life had written very little, and it showed.

Even the fact that she sat here now beside him, his wedding ring upon her finger, knowing so little about him, proved her fatuity. How could anyone marry a stranger on an impulse without even asking him a few pertinent questions? She had allowed him to use her ruthlessly, almost as if she had no will of her own. She despised herself and she disliked and feared him.

Since their marriage he had come no closer, made no demands, showed no alteration in his cool, polite manner. They had had separate rooms at the hotels where they had stayed on their way back to the Limousin. They had spoken together like strangers.

She felt the whole situation to be bizarre, unbelievable.

Once, talking over dinner, her face flushed with

wine, she had mentioned Hal and broken off the
sentence, distress in her face. Philippe had watched
her narrowly.

'Forget him,' he advised sharply.

'We were engaged for a year,' she said, her mouth
trembling. 'It isn't that easy.'

'Where's your pride?' He looked scornful. 'I would
never let a woman linger in my mind once she had
proved herself a cheat.'

Alex had looked at him, reading his hard, cold face,
and shivered. No, she had thought, he would have no
compunction in hurting back, in completely destroying
if he decided to, in shutting off love as if it had never
existed. 'Lucky you,' she had said.

'You do not mean that,' he said, his accent very
French, a dark frown on his face. The grey eyes considered her. 'You do not like me much, do you, Alex?'

She had flushed. 'Was that part of our bargain?'

'I merely wanted to hear you say it,' he said drily.
'You said it very clearly the night you were in my
room. The champagne loosened that tongue of yours. I
prefer the truth. I cannot bear lies.'

'Neither can I,' she agreed.

'I'm glad to hear it,' he said.

Then she had said suddenly, 'Although this is all a
lie, isn't it? Our marriage, I mean. A charade intended
to impress this woman who doesn't even love you ...
so you're not so honest, after all, are you, Philippe?'

His face had been blank. After a moment he had
smiled coldly. 'Even a charade is preferable to hurt
pride, I suppose.'

Now, turning to look at him curiously, as they drove
along a high-banked narrow lane between deep woods,
she asked him, 'Shall I meet this mysterious girl who

is the reason for my being here?'

For a second or two he stared at her expressionlessly, then he lifted his shoulders in a Gallic shrug. 'Even if you did, I would prefer you knew nothing about it. Your face is too easy to read. You could never disguise your thoughts. That is why I had to make such a big performance out of breaking your engagement. Alone, you could never have convinced your fiancé that you were in love with someone else.'

'Why didn't you tell me that Deirdre wasn't the first woman in his life?' she asked him, suddenly finding it odd that he had kept that from her. 'If I'd known what a flirt he was I wouldn't have cared how I broke the engagement. I would just have told him to drop dead.'

'Would you?' His mouth quirked sardonically. 'I wonder. You are far too soft, Alex, to be ruthless. He would have talked you round, persuaded you it was all a mistake, got you to believe he truly loved you. You had to break the engagement before you really saw him clearly.'

'You're totally ruthless, aren't you?' she asked, her green eyes anxious. 'Why am I letting you push me around like this? I need my head examined!'

He laughed softly. 'We are opposites, you and I, wouldn't you say? But that is no reason why a marriage between us should not work.'

'So long as I remember who gives the orders,' she said wryly.

He laughed again, his grey eyes mocking. 'What man does not wish to be master in his own house?'

'I've no doubt you are,' she said ruefully, eyeing him. Master in his own house ... oh, she had no doubts at all. It was stamped on every tough, ruthless inch of him.

The car spun round a wooded corner and came through a tall gate marked by square posts on which were set elaborately carved pineapples of cream stone. Alex sat up straight and stared as the car slowly drove down the long white road and she watched in disbelief, shock and horror as the turreted castle grew closer and closer. Philippe glanced at her, his brows level. The colour had all left her face and she had clenched her hands in her lap, the fingers taut.

'That is Sarconne,' he said, in a voice which had grown deep with feeling.

'Stop the car,' she said hoarsely, moving as though she would jump out if he did not.

The car braked and stood still abruptly, sending her falling. He bent to help her and she pushed him away, then turned a white, angry face towards him.

'Why didn't you tell me? How dare you keep it a secret? How could you do this to me?'

'If I'd told you, would you have married me?' he asked drily.

'No,' she said desperately.

'Then you know why I didn't tell you,' he said.

She was shattered. 'I said you were ruthless,' she said wildly. 'But this ... is damnable, bringing me here unprepared, without an idea what I was to see. I can't do it! Take me back to London, Philippe. I can't go through with this ... how could you imagine I would be able to? A place like this ... I would be wildly out of my depth, unable to cope. I'm not the sort of wife you need.' The words were pouring out, incoherent, bitter, terrified. The green eyes had a feverish glaze, a look of sheer misery, and her face was quite white.

He listened calmly, his face unmoved. When her words at last ended with a sob, he said, 'You are my wife. Nothing now will alter that. Pull yourself together. What is so terrible?' He took out a handkerchief and began to wipe the tearstains from her face with a gentle hand. Producing a comb, he tidied her hair, his eyes on her white face. 'Do something about your make-up,' he ordered, and, like an automaton, she obeyed. He put a finger under her chin and inspected her calmly. 'Good. Now you look as ravishing as ever,' he said.

Her green eyes were bitter. 'Ravishing!' The word was flung back furiously.

'Yes, didn't you know?' He grinned at her. 'You're far too modest, chérie. You have a great beauty, but most of the time it is submerged beneath your quiet manner ... just now and then it breaks free. As it did the first time we met when you were walking on the groyne and laughing into the face of the wind ... then you looked wild and untamed, like a spirit. When I saw you in the hotel that bright, wild look had gone, and there was a placid, submissive creature in a black dress. You puzzled me. You still do.'

'Don't think I don't know what you're doing,' Alex snapped angrily.

'What am I doing?' His brows arched curiously.

'Trying to get me to do just what you want me to do,' she said resentfully. 'I'm beginning to know you now. You can charm the birds off the trees when you choose!'

'Even you, Alex?' he asked mockingly, looking into her eyes with a slight smile.

A flush crept into her cheeks. 'Nothing in my life has

made me fit to have a place like this as my home,' she protested. 'It's not my element at all.'

'We shall see about that,' Philippe said coolly. 'I say you shall be mistress of Sarconne.' The grey eyes held her glance. 'Are you offering to defy me, Alex?'

'Why me?' she asked, her glance falling away. 'Now that I've seen it I'm sure you could have married anyone you liked. Why did you do it?'

'I saw a girl defying the wind and the waves,' he said lightly. 'A girl who could do that could defy anything, surely, Alex.'

She turned and looked towards the castle, shivering. 'Not that place.'

'You don't like Sarconne?' He sounded wry.

'Like it? It's beautiful,' she cried angrily. 'Far too beautiful. It frightens me.'

He turned her head, holding it between both hands, his eyes finding hers. 'I am master of Sarconne and you are my wife,' he said levelly. 'When you enter it, Alex, you will remember that, and remember that I expect you to act like my wife from now on ... everyone will be watching you. You will look like a bride and you will act like one.'

'What is that supposed to mean?' she asked, her fear growing.

'This,' he said, bending forward.

She had had no premonition to warn her. She sat, startled and incredulous, as Philippe's mouth found her lips. For a few seconds with widening eyes and a sense of disbelief she sat very still, feeling the hard, sensual curve of his mouth warming her, then his arms came round her, pulling her across the car, and a deep, probing exploration came into the kiss. She had had little experience of men. Her years in the hotel trade had meant long hours and restricted company. She had been kissed before with passion—Hal had never pressed her to abandon her principles, but he had been an ardent lover. But never before had any man kissed her the way Philippe was kissing her now, and she was shaken and disturbed by the reaction of her own body.

When he released her and moved away she straightened, her cheeks very pink, her mouth quivering and stinging from the violence of his kiss, her eyes dazed.

'Now you look like a bride,' Philippe said with satisfaction, starting the engine.

The kiss had so shaken her that she barely felt anything as they drove down towards the castle. It was square built, with round towers at each corner, their tops conical. The main gate was entered over a lowered drawbridge. As the car rattled over the wooden slats Alex peered to one side and saw the dry moat, grassed smoothly.

Slowly her eyes moved up to the hard stone surround of the gatehouse, carved with shields whose devices time had eaten away in places, and above that the soaring height of the building. They drove under the gateway into an inner courtyard canopied by the blue sky, and she began to tremble helplessly.

Philippe laid a hand upon her thigh, taking her by surprise. She looked round at him, her green eyes enlarged by fear, and he said quietly, 'Lift up your head, Alex. You are a new bride, remember.'

He got out of the car, came round and opened the door for her, his grey eyes steady on her face as he helped her to descend.

When Alex pictured this homecoming she had vaguely imagined a house in some French village or

town, perhaps close to a vineyard. The little Philippe
had let fall had given her the impression that his house
was old, but that it should be so huge, so old, so lovely
had never entered her head.

Her fingers crushed by his, she lifted her red-gold
head in a gesture of pride, her green eyes wary. She was
wearing a dress he had bought in Paris, a delicate cream
silk which clung to her slender body, outlining every
curve, softening the bright gleam of her hair.

There were two people standing by an open door,
watching them closely. Philippe drew her towards
them, his hand beneath her elbow.

'My brother Gaston,' he said. 'And his wife, Elise.'

Alex looked from one to the other quickly, taking in
what she could of them at a quick glance, then held out
her hand politely to her new brother-in-law as he
stepped towards her.

'We were astonished by Philippe's cable,' he said
softly. 'But now that I see you, I'm no longer surprised.'

She flushed and heard him laugh quietly. The next
moment he took hold of her shoulders, kissed her
quickly on each cheek with a Gallic gesture, smiled
down into her nervous face, then bent his head and
kissed her quite deliberately on the mouth. He took his
time, enjoying it, but without any real pressure, and as
he stepped back his black eyes held a teasing little
smile.

Alex felt an answering amusement, all her instincts
telling her that he, at least, liked her. Her smile deepened warmly, her eyes holding a friendly smile.

Philippe's hand had seized her by the waist in the
next second. She felt his fingers digging into her
brutally, and looked sidelong at him, surprised and
annoyed. Surely he didn't object to his brother kissing

her? she thought. Meeting the frosty grey eyes, she gave him a mischievous smile, a flirtatious, provocative flutter of her lashes. He had said he wanted to convince everyone that they were an ordinary newly wed couple, so she might as well play the part properly.

'You aren't jealous of your own brother, darling!' she said lightly.

Philippe stared into her face, his eyes narrowing. For a second he looked dangerous, a man who could be frightening. Then he tightened his grip on her and said softly, 'Just don't let Gaston make a habit of it, *mignonne*!'

The watching woman laughed coldly. 'Gaston has always made a habit of kissing women,' she said in brittle tones. 'Too late to change him now.'

Alex slowly took in Gaston's wife; the petite, rounded figure, the silver-blonde hair, the slanting, malicious blue eyes. Elise was much older than herself —nearly thirty, she guessed, more or less the same age as her husband. The two of them made a striking couple. Gaston was as dark as his brother, thinner, less powerful, less commanding. His features had an almost effeminate beauty, sculptured into well-moulded lines, the fine-boned face slightly melancholic, touched with strain. His blonde wife made the perfect foil for him. She glittered in white and black, elegant and self-assured.

When Alex offered her hand, Elise touched the fingers coldly. She ran her blue eyes over Alex's face and figure, her brows lifted. 'Welcome to Sarconne,' she said icily. Then she looked at Philippe. 'This is very sudden, Philippe. We were taken by surprise.'

'It took us by surprise, too,' he said politely. 'I am sure you will welcome my wife to Sarconne, though.'

The words were spoken very softly, but with an under-lying note which almost seemed to Alex to hold menace, although such a thought was ridiculous.

'Of course,' said the high, brittle voice. 'Did you have a good journey, Alex?'

'Yes, thank you,' Alex said mutedly.

Gaston asked his brother a question and while Philippe answered Alex curiously looked around her. The four sides of the chateau surrounded them as they stood in the large courtyard. In the centre of it stood a fountain which played gently in the sunlight, sending a cool trickle of water down into a scalloped shell with a melodic little sound. There was a colonnade around the four sides of the rectangle, the wooden pillars painted white, meeting curved sills overhead. Flowers spilled from the sills, splashing the scarlet and white of their petals into the sunlit air. Leaded windows climbed up on all sides, reflecting the sun.

Gaston moved to Alex's side and smiled at her. 'When the chateau was built this made a convenient place for the ladies to walk in,' he explained.

Alex nodded with interest. 'It's very beautiful,' she said, suppressing the fear Sarconne bred in her. The weight of all that history, of all that power, seemed to fall upon her mind, crushing her personality.

'How old are you, Alex?' Gaston asked, studying her with a curiously wry smile.

'Twenty-two,' she said, flushing.

He lifted his thin dark brows. 'You have an un-touched look,' he said, almost as if he spoke to himself. 'I thought you were younger.'

They were standing apart from the other two and, as if Elise resented it, she said, 'I've no doubt Alex will wish to rest after the drive. I will show her to her room.'

'I'll do that,' Philippe said abruptly. There was a possessive note in his voice, a possessive movement in the hand which descended on Alex's arm. She knew he was merely doing it to make their marriage convincing, but she felt herself blush as he led her away.

Gaston and Elise followed them into the house. They passed through a tall, carved oak door into a great hall which seemed to Alex to be filled with shadows. Panelled in ancient, polished oak which time had blackened, it had leaded windows set high in the walls from which light fell dimly.

'We will see you again later,' Gaston said as Philippe led her towards a small stone-framed door.

Alex threw him a warm, backward smile, sensing a sadness in him which appealed to a similar sadness in herself, and his black eyes smiled back at her.

They walked up wide stairs, the treads creaking under their feet, and she shivered. How many dead feet had passed up and down before them, people of whom she knew nothing, to whom she would be nothing? She felt herself to be an impostor whose presence here under such circumstances would be resented by the dead of Sarconne.

'Who else lives in the house?' she asked Philippe's averted profile. 'You've told me nothing about your family.'

'Apart from Gaston and Elise, there is nobody,' he said calmly, opening a door.

As he stood back she walked past him and halted in her tracks, backing like a frightened animal as her eyes took in what lay before her. She found him at her back, his hands on her thin shoulders, holding her, controlling her nervous quivering.

'This is our room,' he said softly.

For a moment she was too busy staring around it, trying to believe what she saw. It would, she thought, be like trying to sleep in some magnificent showplace.

She had never stood in such a room. Opulent, palatial, it terrified her. Suddenly her brain made sense of what Philippe had just said and she froze, turning, her eyes flashing angrily to his watchful face. 'What did you say?'

'This is our room,' he repeated coolly, his mouth quizzical.

'No,' she gasped, a shocked instant later. 'I won't ... you can't ...'

'You will and I can,' he said drily, laughing at her.

She backed away slowly, the beauty and terror of the room forgotten in this new shock. 'When we got married you said it was just a charade, a pretence.'

'But it isn't,' he said softly, advancing, his grey eyes mocking her look of alarm.

'You don't think I'd let you . . .' She broke off huskily, still backing from him.

She had reached the bed, the great fourposter which dominated the room, with its high, scalloped canopy and the ornate gilt bedhead carved and adorned with a coat of arms, the blue silk brocade of curtains and covers glowing in jewel-like brilliance. There was an embroidered tapestry on the wall behind it, gilded columns supporting the stucco ceiling above. Her wide, terror-stricken eyes caught her own reflection in the vast, gilt-edged mirror which hung on the wall opposite. She looked like a phantom in the silken room, her face white, her green eyes enormous.

Philippe put his hands on her shoulders and gently

pushed. She was so off balance that she fell backwards with a muffled cry and found herself lying on the silken bedcover, Philippe beside her, his long hands holding her immobile.

'Let me go,' she whispered shakily. 'What sort of girl do you think I am?'

'A trusting, naïve little idiot,' he said wryly.

'I won't let you lay a finger on me,' she protested, her colour rising. 'I should have known you would try something like this!'

His eyes filled with laughter. 'You should,' he agreed. 'You should indeed. You were too busy yearning for your ex-fiancé to think straight, weren't you, Alex? You should try thinking some time. It helps with the little problems of life.'

She struggled against his controlling hands, her eyes flaming with bitterness. 'Let me go!'

He stared down into her face, his hands on her shoulders, his grey eyes flicking over her, a curious smile on his hard mouth.

'Did you really think I intended our marriage to be a hollow one?' he asked her almost curiously. 'You little fool!'

'A fool to believe a word you ever said to me!' she exclaimed furiously.

'I told you the truth,' he said derisively. 'As far as it went. You didn't ask, and I didn't tell you, that I intended our marriage to be some sort of platonic relationship. I'm a man, not a boy scout.'

'I don't care what you intend,' she said wildly. 'Will you let me go or do I have to scream this place down?'

He laughed and the dark head bent towards her, his lips silencing her before she had a chance to carry out her threat.

The first bruising impact of his mouth hurt her, as if he were angry with her for some reason, forcing her lips to part for him in a fierce, possessive movement she could not refuse. She made a wild, futile effort to evade him, twisting in his arms, her slender body trembling, and he laughed harshly against her mouth, insisting that she lie still, his hands forceful. She stared at him, seeing his face too close for comfort, the hard angles of cheekbones and forehead, the glinting grey eyes, the tough chin. Then his mouth came down hard, searching now for response rather than enforcing capitulation, and she could not keep her eyes open. The light hurt. She felt an inexplicable desire to hide, although from what she did not know. She was pulled nearer, her breasts crushed by his body, and for the first time in her life was pulled into a wild whirlpool of sensation. She had never known that a kiss could imply so much of taking and giving, of shared sensuality. A dangerous flare of need lit in her mind. She went limp, curving closer to the hard male body, and felt his hands begin to move over her. When his hands slid the buttons of her dress out of their buttonholes she protested weakly, pushing him away, but he silently persisted, and when his fingers found their way to the smooth surface of her skin she groaned with muffled distress. 'Please ... don't!'

'I want you,' he said, his mouth suddenly moving tenderly over her breast. 'You're so beautiful.'

'No,' she muttered, shivering.

'Of course you are beautiful,' he said, laughing.

'I meant ... no,' she whispered, flushing, then flushed more deeply under the mocking grey eyes.

'I know what you meant,' he teased. 'But what sort of husband would accept no from his wife?'

'I'm not,' she cried incoherently.

'What's this, then?' he asked, lifting her hand and forcing her to see the gold wedding ring he had placed on her finger only a few days earlier.

'Just a pretence,' she said wildly.

'It is perfectly legal,' he said, tongue in cheek, watching the heated little face. 'I married you and now I want my wife.'

'Let me go,' she whispered, struggling against those cruel, demanding hands. 'Please!'

He held her firmly, the grey eyes sliding over her, and she became deeply aware of the expression in them as they observed her. No man had ever looked at her like that before. Philippe forced her to be aware of her body and his own response to it. Even worse, he forced her to be aware of her unbidden response to him.

'I can't,' she said huskily. 'Not without love.'

His mouth mocked her. 'Don't you enjoy it when I do this, Alex?' He began to kiss the side of her neck, his lips cool on her hot skin.

She was angry to find she did like it. When Hal kissed her it had never aroused these warm tides of sensuality inside her. Philippe's caresses were sending shivers of pleasure down her spine.

There was a tap on the door. Alex jumped, but Philippe held her, one hand curved over the warm, naked swell of her breast. 'Who is it?' he asked curtly.

'Elise,' a voice replied, and the door opened.

Alex was so embarrassed that she turned her head to one side, closing her eyes. There was a silence. Then Philippe said sardonically, 'We are very busy, Elise. Whatever it was can wait.'

There was no answer, but the door slammed suddenly, and Philippe laughed.

The sound of his laughter was grimly mocking. Alex turned her head to stare at him in dismay and surprise. He was staring at the door with a curious look on his face. And then Alex guessed what she should have guessed long ago. Elise was the other woman ... the woman who had chosen another man and who had to be shown that Philippe did not care.

CHAPTER THREE

PHILIPPE turned his head and their eyes met. 'What's the matter?' he asked her. 'You look petrified.' His frown deepened. 'There's no need to panic,' he drawled derisively. 'I'm not going to force you to do anything. Rape has never fascinated me. Sooner or later you'll be willing, and I can wait.'

Alex's colour rose alongside her temper. 'Oh, sooner or later I'll be willing, will I? My God, you think a lot of yourself! Does it occur to you that I may find you repulsive?'

He laughed, giving her a teasing look. 'No, and don't tell me you do, because I wouldn't believe it!'

'I'm sure you wouldn't,' she snapped. 'Your conceit is quite impregnable, isn't it?'

'Not my conceit,' he said coolly, leaning back on one elbow. 'My experience tells me that you find me attractive. You can't hide a thing like that, my dear, when you are this close.' And he rolled nearer, his eyes an inch away from hers, his mouth almost touching her lips. Alex felt a swimming sensation in her head, a peculiar feeling as if she might be going to faint. Her eyes widened, then fell before his stare, while she waited for the kiss, her breath quickening.

He laughed softly. 'You see what I mean?' he asked.

She flung away, turning on to her stomach, plucking at the coverlet with nervous fingers.

'I not only don't like you,' she said huskily, 'I don't trust you an inch. You let me think Hal actually loved someone else when you knew all the time it was just another flirtation.'

'I see,' he drawled coldly. 'Had you known, you would have turned a blind eye, would you?'

'I told you,' she snapped. 'I would have had no qualms about walking out on him without a word, if I'd known.'

'No qualms?' His voice was sharp.

Her lip trembled and she put her face into her hands. 'Oh, shut up!' The thought of Hal burnt inside her like a red-hot poker in thin gauze. After so long how could she be expected to forget him overnight? she asked herself.

'He was a selfish, conceited swine,' Philippe told her harshly. 'Do you think I don't know you've thought of him ever since we left that damned hotel? I'm beginning to recognise the look on your face which says you are thinking of him. Your eyes get a stupid dreamy look in them and your whole face goes soft ... my God, have you no pride? Learn to put him out of your head before it is too late.'

'Are you sure you really love this woman?' she asked cruelly, turning to glare at him, her green eyes wet with tears. 'I don't think you know the first thing about love. All you want is your revenge!'

'Who said anything about revenge?' he asked, his face growing furious.

'Oh, you said it was to salve your pride,' she agreed scornfully. 'But I saw your face just now after she saw us together, and you were delighted that she'd come in and seen us. I guessed as soon as I saw her. You hoped seeing me in your arms would hurt her, didn't you? Is that what you call love?'

There was a silence. He stared at her, his face quite

blank, the hard grey eyes unreadable.

'Did you think I wouldn't guess?' she asked him. 'Oh, I can understand how you feel, to have your own brother marry the woman you want, but don't expect me to let you make love to me just to satisfy your ego and hurt her.'

His voice was flat. 'To be frank, my dear, I don't give a damn why you sleep with me, but sleep with me you will, sooner or later. It's time you came to terms with the fact that we're husband and wife, for whatever reason, and I don't intend my marriage to be some sort of platonic ritual. I want a woman in my bed, not a dreaming adolescent.'

'You tricked me!' she flung, flushing at his insult. 'Why weren't you honest about everything? You never mentioned the fact that you lived in a damned great castle ...'

'Sarconne is not a castle,' he drawled coldly. 'It is a chateau, a fortified house, if you like.' He slapped her suddenly, without violence, a friendly slap. 'Stop quarrelling with me on your first day in Sarconne. Get changed and come and look at it with me. It is to be your home, after all.'

'You're joking,' she said bitterly. 'One look from your family and I knew I was an outsider.'

'My wife is not an outsider,' he said. 'Don't be idiotic.'

'What do I even know about you? I spilled out everything to you. You told me nothing.'

'I wanted to tell you here,' he said. 'This is where it all begins ... this is the Royal Chamber, kept for kings of France to use, during the eighteenth century, but our room now.'

Alex sat up on the bed and looked around the room

at the rich, glowing colours and silken fabrics. 'It's too unreal. I should feel unreal sleeping in it.'

'I will make sure you feel very real indeed,' he murmured.

She looked at him in startled surprise and met taunting grey eyes, feeling heat glowing in her face.

'I was born here,' he added, his hand stroking over the cover.

Her eyes widened. 'Oh!' It was a shattering thought. She stared, trying to imagine him as a baby, a small boy, a growing one ... and failing. He was too powerful, too confident, too assured. Was he ever weak, small, unsure of himself? It was an improbable idea. 'Was your brother born here, too?'

His face was blank. 'Only the masters of Sarconne are born in this room,' he said.

She laughed. 'How can anyone tell in advance whether the baby will be a boy or a girl?'

His eyes were suddenly amused. 'The first child born to our family is always born in this room. If it is a girl it does not count. If it is a boy, all future births take place elsewhere.'

'How simple,' she said sarcastically. 'I shall have my babies in hospital.' Then she flushed bright pink and gasped at herself.

'I will see about that when the time comes,' he murmured softly, looking amused.

'They won't be yours,' she cried furiously.

'They had better be,' he said, his eyes mocking. 'It is a tradition of my house that unfaithful wives are strangled.'

'What about unfaithful husbands?' she asked to cover her embarrassment.

Philippe laughed. 'That is another matter,' he said drily.

'You mean men can do just as they like?'

'They always have,' he shrugged.

'No wonder the French gave the word chauvinist to the world,' she said bitterly.

He eyed her calmly. 'Do you want to hear about my family or don't you?'

'How long have they lived here?'

'Since the seventeenth century,' he said. 'An ancestor of mine married the heiress of the family who built Sarconne—they had been here for generations before that, so in a sense one family has lived here ever since it was built.'

'Which was when?'

'The fourteenth century,' he said. 'It has been altered a good deal since then—the central part of the chateau was built in the eighteenth century, as you will see when we go downstairs. The façade has been restructured several times. Only the towers are original. The first part of Sarconne was the donjon ... we will go and look at it when you are ready.'

'I'm hungry,' she said childishly. 'And tired.'

He looked at her with a sigh. 'Of course. I'm sorry— I had been looking forward to showing you Sarconne.'

'I'm sorry,' she said, feeling guilty at once. 'I will come.' She got off the bed, but Philippe smiled down at her, shaking his head.

'No, you are right. You must have some rest and some food. I can show you Sarconne tomorrow.'

Alex felt like stamping her foot. 'I want to see it now!'

Philippe eyed her curiously. 'How like a woman ... blowing hot, then cold! Come on.' He took her hand

and pulled her towards the door.

They walked along the corridor and passed through a narrow, arched door into a circular room whose plaster ceiling was painted in a pale green picked out with gold. Philippe led her through it and on to a stone staircase which wound up, the handrail only rope chained to the wall at intervals. They climbed upward and emerged on to a narrow catwalk which ran round the large circular tower.

Alex leaned on the stone parapet and stared out over the dark green of the woods, the distant misty fields, the climbing hills.

'It's marvellous!' she breathed.

'Yes,' he said soberly. 'Don't ever come up here on your own, will you, Alex? It could be dangerous.'

'Isn't the tower safe?' she asked in surprise. It looked as solid as eternity, a great edifice of stone which had lasted hundreds of years and would last for ever.

'The donjon,' he said. 'This is the keep of the old castle.'

'Chateau,' she teased.

'When the donjon was built that was all there was,' he said. 'A great tower meant to keep down the peasants. Only when life was more peaceful was the rest of the chateau added.'

'Did your family own all the land then?' she asked, staring over the landscape with admiration.

'Then?' His brows rose. 'We still do . . . most of what you can see, anyway. There are four farms, the vineyards, the factory . . .'

'Factory?' Her face was white. 'You own a factory, too?'

'We manufacture porcelain,' he said. 'It is a fine porcelain of the highest standard, very expensive ...

handmade in the old days, but now some of the process has to be machine operated—the price of progress. We still hand-glaze, hand-paint. The kilns are automatic, though.'

'You're rich,' she said, as if she flung a bitter accusation.

'Does that matter?' he asked, watching her out of narrowed eyes.

'Of course it does,' she snapped, her face angry. 'You know that. Oh, what on earth am I to do? You tricked me!'

'If I had pretended to be rich, then turned out to be poor, your anger would be understandable,' he said drily.

'You pretended to be a man who needed my help,' she said incoherently. 'I thought you were a businessman, maybe an executive ... not a wealthy man with the sort of way of life I've only read of, not come in contact with ... what will your family think when they know you've married a girl without a background, a girl who's worked in hotels all her life and has no money or family?'

'I don't give a damn what they think,' he shrugged. 'It was me you married, not them.'

'That just shows how selfish you are,' she said crossly. 'I've got to live here knowing they all despise me. I'll never be accepted and you know it. I'm outclassed.'

'You will hold your own,' he said levelly.

'How can I?'

'You will have to find a way,' he said.

'You're flinging me into deep water when I don't know how to swim,' she said.

'You will learn or drown,' he shrugged.

'My God, you are a bastard,' she said through her teeth. 'I don't just dislike you. I detest you!'

Philippe was staring at her flushed face, her brilliant angry green eyes, the red-gold hair which the wind from the open woods was blowing into a shimmering halo around her head. An odd smile flickered around his hard mouth.

'Perhaps my opinion of you is higher than your own,' he said drily. 'Come down and change for dinner.'

As they passed back into the main part of the house they met a tall, thin woman in black who gave Philippe a quick, smiling look and stopped. He kissed her warmly on her cheek, then drew Alex forward.

'Lélie, this is Alex,' he said.

Alex looked nervously at her and met dark eyes which smiled and a sharp, shrewd face. 'Alex,' smiled the other woman, kissing her cheeks softly. 'I nursed Philippe from birth, so you will excuse me if I seem to bully him now and then!'

Alex felt herself relax. For the first time since she entered this house she had met someone who did not make her feel an intruder. On an impulse, she said, 'I was wondering earlier whether he was ever a baby. It seems hard to imagine, although he says he was born in the Royal Chamber.'

Lélie laughed. She was about sixty, Alex guessed, although she was very well preserved for her age. Her black hair was coiled around her head in a thin plait. Her skin was sallow and her mouth a little too wide for her thin face. There was humour and warmth in the black eyes, lines of laughter around eyes and mouth.

'He was a very good baby,' she said. 'A little obstinate.'

'That I can believe,' said Alex drily.

'He only cried when he was really angry, and then he roared!'

'Enough is enough,' Philippe said coolly. 'When I have a son of my own I may be prepared to listen to baby talk. Until then, I prefer not to.'

Alex felt herself blush and Lélie laughed again. 'Talking of babies so soon? Now I believe you are married, Philippe!'

'Or is that why he was married so suddenly?' asked a light, cool, malicious voice from the stairs.

Lélie did not turn her head, but Alex saw a cold look come into her face. Philippe turned, however, his eyes narrowing.

'What exactly is that supposed to mean, Elise?'

Elise laughed lightly. 'Oh, I am not old-fashioned enough to be prudish, Philippe. When a man talks of babies within days of his wedding, what else is one to think?'

'I am not pregnant,' said Alex, her voice trembling with indignation. 'I am not ...' She was about to say she was not even a wife yet, but Philippe's hand seized her arm tightly, biting into her flesh so that she turned her head to look at him, a cry of pain on her lips.

'There is no need to upset yourself,' he said. 'Elise did not mean to be offensive.'

'I thought English girls were very permissive these days,' Elise said, laughing.

'Some may be,' Alex said angrily. 'But I am not.'

Elise lifted her brows. 'So Philippe had to marry to get what he wanted, did he? Poor Philippe!'

The hot colour deepened in Alex's face and she looked at Elise with positive hatred. Philippe was saying nothing, watching them both with narrowed eyes.

'Philippe's reasons for marrying me are none of your business,' she said icily, holding herself very straight and tautly. 'You must not imagine that everyone shares your odd code of morals.'

Elise's eyes flashed very blue, rage in them. 'How dare you!'

'If you insult me, I shall reply in kind,' Alex retorted, her mouth tight. Then she turned and walked away back towards her own room, and after a few seconds heard Philippe following her. She went to the window and stared out, quivering with the nervous tension of having argued with Elise.

'Do you want to use the bathroom first?' he asked quietly at her back. 'It is through this door.'

She turned and saw, then, that their cases had been brought up and were lying open on the bed. Someone had unpacked all her things, she saw, glancing into the wardrobe.

Just then a knock at the door made her start nervously. Philippe tersely ordered whoever it was to come in, and a girl came into the room, looking anxiously at them both.

'Excuse me, Monsieur le Comte. Maman asked me to report to Madame la Comtesse,' she said softly.

Alex backed against the window, her trembling hands seizing the windowsill to hold it tightly. For a swimming moment she was afraid she would fall if she did not hold on.

Philippe stared at her white, taut face out of hard eyes. 'My wife does not need you for the moment, Gisèle,' he said calmly. 'You will take up your duties tomorrow.'

There was a brief hesitation, then the girl gave a slight curtsey and went out.

Alex turned her head slowly and stared at him. 'How many more shocks are in store for me?' she asked him in a low, shaking voice. 'How could you?'

'Take it in your stride, Alex,' he said flatly. 'What does a title mean today? I am Philippe de Villone, that is all. I never use my title when I am abroad. I forget it completely.'

'You've made a fool of me,' she said bitterly. 'Coming here, so totally unprepared for all this ... if someone had called me ... what that girl called me just now, I wouldn't have known where to look!'

'So it is lucky it was just Gisèle,' he shrugged.

'Why didn't you tell me?'

'I forgot,' he said.

'Forgot?' She was incredulous.

'It isn't important,' he said. 'Don't let it seem so.'

'That's easy for you to say,' she said. 'How long have you been a comte ... comte of what?'

'Since my father died,' he said patiently. 'I was fourteen. And I am Comte de Sarconne, of course ... what else?'

'What else?' she asked bitterly.

There was a pause, then she asked, 'What did you mean about Gisèle taking up her duties?'

'She is your new maid,' he explained.

She flushed deeply. 'Oh, God!' She turned and laid her face on the cold glass of the window, feeling tears stinging behind her eyes.

'Lélie is her mother,' he said quietly. 'She will be excellent for you—Lélie has trained her very well. She is a kind, sweet-tempered, helpful child. She is just eighteen, so you need not be afraid of her.'

Alex wiped a hand across her eyes, turned, her face rigidly controlled and said slowly, 'I don't think I can go through with this, Philippe. We must get an annulment. I couldn't cope with your family, this place and all the servants ... you shouldn't have done this to me!'

'You will feel better when you've had a bath and a meal,' he said. 'We'll discuss it tomorrow.'

She hesitated a moment too long. Philippe turned and walked out of the room, and after a long pause Alex gathered up a change of clothes and went into the bathroom.

Instinct prompted her to dress as well as she could for this first meal en famille. By the time Philippe returned she had spent twenty minutes on her appearance, carefully piling her red-gold hair into a delicate coronet of curls at the back of her head, giving a soft green shimmer to her lids, outlining her mouth in a beige-pink lipstick. She wore another of the dresses they had bought in Paris—a sea-green confection which glittered metallically as she moved, the bodice curving in over her small, high breasts, yet discreetly veiling her bare shoulders and arms with a matching cape with a silken fringe which swayed as she walked.

Philippe halted, staring at her.

She lifted her head defiantly. 'Will I do?'

'For what?' he asked softly. 'I can think of several things.'

Her cheeks glowed at the implication and she gave him a cold look. 'You're as bad as Elise!'

'And you are as cold as the English weather,' he said, his mouth tight.

'You'll never have the chance to find out,' she snapped.

'We'll see about that,' he murmured, his glance trailing down over her slender body. Then he turned and began to look through his own wardrobe, pulling out a dark suit. 'Wait for me,' he ordered.

Alex sat down on the deep window seat, her heart beating very fast. She felt as if she had a terrible ordeal in front of her.

Suddenly the thought of Hal flashed into her mind and she felt a dart of pain. What was she doing here? Only a fortnight ago she had been rapturously looking forward to her marriage to Hal, sure of their love for each other, knowing exactly what life held for her, dreaming of a pleasant little house, children, an ordinary marriage. Philippe had blown into her life as if the wind had brought him—a powerful dark stranger, turning her secure little world upside down, destroying all her dreams and wrenching her away from her moorings as if she were a fragile craft blown off course by a remorseless wind.

'Oh, Hal,' she whispered brokenly, dropping her face into her trembling hands. One could not just turn love off as if it were a tap. It went on inside one, hurting and bewildering.

Behind her closed lids she saw his kind, smiling face, and then she thought of the moment when she had seen him with another woman in his arms, heard the passion with which he spoke.

How could he have done such things?

He could never have loved her. She faced that with a shiver. A year of lying, deceiving, secrecy ...

It was a bitter thought. She felt humiliated when she imagined how the staff had been smiling behind her back. What a fool she had been!

And Philippe had made a fool of her too. She had married him on a wild, humiliated impulse, partly to get away from the place where she had been made to feel so stupid, partly because he had saved her face, as he had promised, even if only at the expense of her good name. At the time all she had thought of was that she could not bear the muddle Hal had made of her life. Now she realised she was in a much more painful situation. She was an ordinary working girl, without money or family, placed in a position she could never hope to fulfil. Just the thought of acting the role of mistress of this beautiful, terrifying house sent shivers down her back. How could she learn to give orders to servants, behave with the regal composure of Philippe's wife, hear herself addressed as Madame la Comtesse?

I hate him, she thought bitterly. She remembered how she first saw him, on the windswept grey beach in the early morning, when she had thought herself quite alone and given way to the delight of braving the sea and the wind. She had exulted in the freedom of that moment, only to turn and see a strong, dark face watching her ... and fallen, humiliated and off balance.

It had been an omen.

The bathroom door opened and Philippe strolled out, elegant in his dark suit, his hair smoothly brushed, his newly shaved face glowing, his grey eyes cool.

'Ready?' he asked her.

Alex lifted her chin, her mouth taut. 'Yes,' she said, as if she accepted a challenge.

He gave her a long look, then bent and kissed her hands, his dark head bent over them for a moment. 'Madame la Comtesse,' he murmured, giving her an upward, teasing glance.

She felt a bubble of laughter in her chest, her mouth curving in a smile. He was right, she thought. It was stupid to let such a thing disturb her ... what did titles matter these days? They were meaningless.

They walked down the stairs together, hand in hand. Philippe's deliberate pressure gave her a confidence she had never felt before. When they entered the room where the rest of the family were waiting, she held her head high, clinging to his hand as if it were a sheet anchor.

'This is the Salon,' he told her as her eyes flicked admiringly around it. It was a very large, square room, the woodwork a pale creamy ivory picked out in gold, the ceiling ornately painted with allegorical scenes, the half-naked women full-fleshed and rosy, the clouds very pink, the flowers very formal, gilt laurel wreaths framing the whole. Over the hearth hung an enormous mirror framed in a trellised arch of stucco. The carpet was cream embossed with flowers. The furniture was upholstered in pale green velvet.

'Here you are, then,' said Gaston, rising as they moved into the room. His good-looking, thin face was smiling as he met Alex's eyes. 'Come and sit beside me, Alex,' he invited. 'We must get acquainted.'

She looked at Philippe hesitantly.

'She will sit with me,' he said flatly, indicating a chair. She sank down and he took up a position on a square stool beside her, leaning against her lap a little, his whole attitude one of intimacy.

'Still in the honeymoon stage, are we?' Elise asked with barbed mockery. 'How sweet!'

'Don't you remember what it was like?' Alex asked softly, smiling past her at Gaston. 'How long have you been married, Gaston?'

'Too long,' he said lightly, yet with an undertone which was not all humour.

'Oh, thank you,' said Elise, her blue eyes furious,

giving him a cold look before she turned those angry eyes on Alex. 'We've been married for five years, for your information,' she said.

Alex could not repress a look of surprise. She had imagined that they must have married recently, or why should Philippe have wished to show her he did not care? Unless ... her mind leapt to a conclusion, one which had not occurred to her until now. Unless Philippe and Elise had had an affair since Elise married Gaston, and Philippe had decided to end it. Was that it?

'You seem surprised,' Gaston drawled, staring at her. 'Didn't Philippe tell you?'

'Philippe told me very little,' she said honestly, aware of his tension beside her, knowing that he was afraid of just how much she would say. 'Have you any children, Gaston?'

There was a brittle silence. Gaston's thin, handsome face grew sardonic. 'No,' he said. 'We have no children. We are looking to Philippe now to supply the deficiency.'

She turned to glance at Philippe and saw his grey eyes hard in anger. Was Elise incapable of having children? she wondered. Then, with a horrified qualm, was that why Philippe had wanted to marry, after all? Did he want children?

Philippe suddenly began to talk about the factory, asking Gaston some technical questions about the work schedule there, and for the next few moments the topic held them all safely. Gaston got up and went to a long table in the corner, asking if Alex would like an aperitif. She gratefully sipped the drink he gave her, glad to have something to do to occupy her hands and attention.

'What did you do before you were married?' Elise asked suddenly. 'We know nothing about you. Who are your family? Have you any brothers or sisters? Where did you live?' She gave a light laugh. 'See how ignorant we are! Philippe was so sudden, so secretive.'

Philippe turned his glass in his hands. 'I left it to my wife to tell you about herself,' he said quietly, not looking at her.

Alex wondered how much he wanted her to tell them, then with a sense of deep conviction knew she must tell them the entire truth. She would not live a lie.

'My parents died when I was fifteen,' she said quietly. 'I have no relatives in the world. I left school when I was seventeen and got a job in a hotel. It gave me a safe home and a job at the same time. I've worked in hotels ever since.'

There was a long silence. Elise laughed softly, eyeing her with catlike amusement. 'What is this, a Cinderella story?'

Before Alex could answer, a servant announced dinner, and they all rose to troop into the Salle-à-Manger. Philippe quietly seated Alex at one end of the leather-embossed dining table, taking the chair opposite himself.

She looked down curiously at the surface of the table, her hand softly stroking the smooth brown leather. 'What an unusual dining table,' she commented, looking at Gaston.

'It was made during the Napoleonic War,' he told her, smiling back at her. 'These nails are supposed to be gold, but I think, myself, that they are probably only iron coated with gilt. We have never tested them, though—the story makes a good anecdote.'

Alex was served with a creamy soup with a bland

taste and was glad to concentrate on it, aware of the conversation which went on between the other three. The servants moved discreetly around the room in the background.

'From tomorrow I shall, of course, turn over the household books and keys to you,' Elise said suddenly, her eyes cold.

Alex looked up, startled and dismayed. 'Oh, there's no need ... I couldn't ...'

Philippe looked down the table at her, his face unyielding. 'You must take up the reins some day,' he said coolly. 'The sooner the better. Elise will help you at first, then you can soon take charge of your own home alone.' His words firmly underlined the situation, bringing a flush of anger into Elise's beautiful cold face.

'And what do you want Gaston and myself to do?' Elise asked him sharply.

'The Dower House is in good order,' said Philippe, his eyes expressionless.

Alex was horrified. Was he truly intending to turn his brother and Elise out of the chateau? Her lips parted to protest, but as if he sensed her dismay, he silently shot a cold glance at her, and she closed her mouth on her unuttered words.

Gaston spoke instead, his voice bland. 'It is the tradition at Sarconne, Elise. The new bride takes everything. You have been lucky that Philippe took so long to choose himself a wife.'

'There is plenty of time,' Philippe said calmly. 'It will take a week or two to sort things out, I imagine.'

Elise turned her blonde head to stare at him. Alex could not see the expression on her face, but she could see Philippe, and she had no difficulty in reading the hard grey eyes as they rested on Elise; cynical mockery, derision, cold rejection in them. She winced. Philippe was determined to hurt as much as he could. How could he claim to love Elise when he could treat her like this? God help any woman who fell in love with this cold, hurtful man. He would flail them with the bitter scorn of his nature if they fell below the standards he set for a woman.

Elise suddenly jumped up, her chair falling over, and ran out of the room. Gaston went on eating as though nothing had happened. The servants quietly picked up the chair, replacing it. Philippe poured himself another glass of wine and sipped it, his eyes cool.

Somehow Alex forced herself to go on eating. Gaston turned and spoke lightly to her. She was sure that he was as well aware of the underlying situation between his brother and his wife as she was—but he seemed impervious to it, as if he cared nothing for Elise.

After dinner, pleading a headache, she went up to bed and quickly undressed, sliding between the sheets, wondering if she could get to sleep before Philippe joined her.

She had no intention of allowing him to make their marriage a real one, but her reactions that afternoon had shocked her into recognising that she did not altogether find his advances unpleasant.

She grimaced, shivering. Why was she trying to fool herself? He might be a cold devil, but he had had no difficulty in arousing her that afternoon, and she did not trust herself to hold him off if he became determined.

The night was warm. She lay in bed, stifling, until at last she got up and went to the window, trying to open it with the sash cords. After a struggle, it slid up and the cool night air rushed into the room. Alex knelt on the sill, breathing deeply.

Her ears picked up the sounds of voices on the terrace below. She peered down into the darkness and with a leap of the heart recognised Philippe and Elise.

'Do you think I don't know why you married her?' Elise asked bitterly. 'Why did it have to be a little nobody like that? Who is she, after all? That vulgar red hair, those eyes ... like a cat's. I suppose she caught your fancy over there, you took her to bed a few times, and then she blackmailed you into marrying her?'

'She is my wife,' Philippe said tightly. 'That is all anyone needs to know. If she doesn't receive the respect due to my wife someone will pay for it, I promise you.' His voice held an icy, menacing tone.

'Oh, if you brought home a mongrel bitch and ordered the servants to call it Madame la Comtesse, I've no doubt they would obey you,' Elise hissed. 'You've always had your own way at Sarconne, Philippe. Except with me!'

Alex did not wait to hear another word. She whirled away from the window and flung herself on the silken bed, her mind in deep confusion, her face white with rage and pain. A mongrel bitch, she thought furiously. How dare she call me that?

A little voice reminded her of Elise's last words ... Philippe had not had his way with her ... what exactly did that mean? She clenched her small hands into fists. As if she couldn't guess! Wasn't that exactly why he had married her, to punish Elise for refusing him? How could he try to seduce his brother's wife? It was despicable of him. And Elise, for all her refusal, seemed as interested in him as he was in her.

She lay in the darkness boiling with temper, swayed

by a desire to show all of them that she was not a nobody whom they could push around and dismiss lightly.

When Philippe walked into the room a while later he halted, peering through the gloom towards her. 'Why are you lying on the bed instead of in it?' he asked in surprise. 'Can't you sleep?'

'No,' she said tightly, restraining herself with an effort. She wanted to burst out with what she had overheard, but she could not bring herself to talk about it.

'I won't be a moment,' he said, disappearing into the bathroom. Alex stared at the ceiling, taut with rage. I hate him, she thought savagely. My God, he's contemptible! He had used her as if she were a wooden doll he bought in an idle moment, bringing her blind into the tormented situation at Sarconne, and pride stung her bitterly.

She watched him walk towards her in his dressing-gown, her green eyes brilliant with loathing.

He sank down beside her and his hand ruffled her loose red hair, his eyes glittering into hers. 'Were you waiting for me, Alex?' he asked, his voice oddly husky.

'Don't touch me,' she spat, sitting up. 'I can't stand having your hands on me!'

There was a little silence. 'What's the matter now?' he asked quite patiently. 'Have you been sitting up here brooding?'

'I've been sitting up here thinking what a swine you are,' she told him furiously. 'I hate the very sight of you!'

'Just as well it's dark, then,' he said in a curiously flat voice. 'You won't be able to see me as I make love to you.'

'You lay a finger on me and I'll slap your head off,' she told him with grim determination.

'Your eyes shine in the dark like a cat's,' he said, laughter in his voice.

'I can scratch like a cat, too,' she threatened.

'Show me,' he invited, still amused, and before she could move his hands caught her by the shoulders and dragged her towards him, struggling every inch of the way.

'Let me go, you bastard!' she hissed.

His head bent over her. She caught the silvery glitter of his eyes for a few seconds before his mouth forced back her head, parting her lips hungrily, as if he had been waiting all evening to taste them beneath his own. For a moment she resisted strongly, trying to free herself, pulling back from the demanding lips. Then something totally unexpected happened inside her, a weakness turning her body to a traitorous response she could no longer control.

His mouth was arousing pulses she had not known she possessed, sending a jungle rhythm pounding along her veins. Her body relaxed helplessly in his arms, her head tilted back to receive the long, drugging kiss. His hands freed her and moved down over the silk of her nightdress, exploring the curved shape of her body, sliding in a smooth caress over breasts, waist, hips. She felt as if she had vertigo, her head spinning dizzily, and clutched at his shoulders to stop herself from falling. His mouth left her parted lips and softly brushed over her cheek to her throat. As if she could offer no resistance, she let her head fall back, and groaned as his lips began to cover her neck and shoulders with light kisses.

His arms came round her, lowering her to the bed.

Nothing in her life had prepared her for the heat of the desire which was filling her. She let her hands slide round his neck and twine into his dark hair; meeting the hard pressure of his mouth eagerly. She had forgotten everything, her mind a total blank, her body in complete control of her responses.

Philippe muttered huskily in French as he caressed her, his face buried between her breasts. The wind blew gently in her loosened hair. She groaned, feeling the fierce demand of the hard body as it moved against her. What am I doing? her brain asked suddenly, and she tried to pull away, driven into panic and fear.

'No!' she cried out wildly, pushing at the wide shoulders, finding with a shocked pang that they were quite naked above her.

'Ssh!' he muttered hoarsely. '*Chérie* ... ssh!'

'I can't,' she muttered, shivering under the arousing hands as they moved over her. 'I've never ...' She broke off, her face deeply flushed.

Philippe held her face between his palms, gazing down into the terrified green eyes. A peculiar tenderness lay in the grey depths of his own eyes. 'You didn't have to tell me that, Alex,' he said huskily. 'Do you think I don't know?'

She bit her lip, shuddering. 'Please, Philippe!' No image of Hal came between them. Her mind was dominated by the hard, sensual face above her, by the compelling body of this stranger who was her husband. She tried to think of Elise, of what she had just overheard, but the poison had lost its power at this moment. They might have been alone in the world. He held her captive, without force, merely by the spell of his physical presence.

'I won't hurt you,' he promised. 'Don't fight me,

Alex. Don't make me take you. Give yourself to me.'

She trembled weakly, her hands pushing at his bare skin. The husky deep voice echoed on inside her brain. She tried to make sense of what he had said, but then his mouth was on hers again, with an erotic intensity which swept aside all other thoughts and feelings. She gasped, her hands closing on his shoulders, swamped by the urgent pleasure of his kiss, then abandoned everything, clinging to him, returning his kiss hungrily, her arms wound round his neck. Moments later she was unaware of anything but the need to give herself to him, satisfy the hard drive of his demand, her untaught body trembling as he took it over the borders of pleasure into fulfilment.

CHAPTER FOUR

ALEX turned sleepily on her pillows, waking to the bright summer morning with a start, then felt a fierce jolt as memory flashed back. Hurriedly her lids rose, searching for him, but she was alone in the bed, only the tumbled sheets providing a witness to what had happened last night.

Her eyes opened to their widest, as green as grass, taking in the Royal Chamber, with all its sumptuous, languorous colours. It had a dreamlike improbability, even though the brilliance of the tapestry had faded with the touch of time and the gilding on the fluted columns was softened to a gentle gleam.

As her eyes swivelled around the room taking in the details again her mind was feverishly summoning back the previous day, and she gave a stifled groan.

The successive hammer blows which had disturbed her yesterday came crashing down in memory, and she covered her face with trembling hands.

She could not bear it! Waking in this room morning after morning, a prisoner in some wild, overstructured dream until she herself became as unreal as her surroundings.

Until she met Philippe her life had been so quiet and ordinary. She felt as if she had wandered into a hall of mirrors, her own reflection thrown back at her, contorted and twisted to unfamiliarity, and with no escape route possible.

Her eyes fixed on the mirror opposite. It held the

burning blue of the sky outside the window, and she stared at it intently, remembering her own emotions during the previous night. A flush grew in her cheeks and she sat up straight in the bed, her slender body stiff, her hands clenched.

Unreal? she thought bitterly. Philippe had mockingly told her he would make her feel very real, and he had meant it. She closed her eyes, pressing her palms over the lids as if to force back the rush of hot tears.

How could she have let him make love to her like that? Was she mad?

It had meant nothing to him—how could it? Her face burned with self-disgust. It had meant nothing to her, either, she told herself bitterly. She didn't even like him. He was as hard as steel, a cold autocrat who rode roughshod over everyone who might get in his way.

Yet, in a matter of moments, he had swept aside her moral prohibition, the simple code by which she had always lived, demanding surrender coolly as though he had every right to do so, and, far from treating him with angry contempt, she had yielded like a willing victim, and, much as she wanted to pretend to herself that she had loathed every moment of it, she admitted furiously that, if she allowed herself to remember anything which had happened between them, she would not find the memory as distasteful as she would wish.

Why had it never occurred to her that this idiotic marriage was bound to hold such traps? Her mouth tightened. He had known what she thought. Aware of her naive belief that their marriage was a pretence, he had planned his course carefully. Why was she such a fool?

She was so disgusted with herself she could have

screamed. She did feel like doing so for a moment, wondering if it might make this glorious charade of a room feel more lifelike.

Then there was a discreet tap on the door. 'Who is it?' she called, looking around for a wrap.

'Gisèle, madame,' came the soft French voice.

She was relieved. 'Come in, Gisèle.'

The girl came in then, her thin young face smiling, and the two girls looked at each other across the room. 'May I run your bath for you, madame?' Gisèle asked hopefully.

Alex was about to laugh and say she could easily run her bath for herself, then she caught herself back, realising that if she allowed Gisèle to do so, she could quickly learn the way the family expected her to behave. 'Thank you, Gisèle,' she said, smiling.

She slid out of the silken bed and wandered across to the window, staring out over the misty landscape. The sun was just breaking through opalescent cloud, turning the colourless sky to a tender blue in places.

'Which dress shall I lay out for you, madame?' Gisèle asked behind her.

Alex was uncertain. She looked vaguely at the other girl. 'Oh, the dark blue one, I think.' It was elegantly noncommittal and would adapt to any occasion.

Gisèle deftly slid it out from the wardrobe, smiling approval. Alex went through to the bathroom and closed the door. The air was filled with scented sweetness and steam. At least in here she felt safe, relaxed, free from the oppression of her surroundings. She deliberately took her time, her eyes closed, soaking in the warm, fragrant water.

Gisèle was a very nice girl, she decided later, as she dressed and talked to her. It was obvious that she was eager to be helpful, offering admiration, not antagonism, and Alex was grateful to have found a friend in this alien world.

'Wouldn't you rather work somewhere exciting, like Paris, Gisèle?' she asked, eyeing herself glumly in the mirror. The dark blue dress did at least make her look slightly more mature, she decided.

Gisèle stood back to gaze at her, smiling. 'I would miss Sarconne,' she said calmly. 'It is my home.'

Alex smiled at her, envying the simple statement. 'Yes, I can imagine that that would make a difference. It is a lovely spot.'

'It has a hold on the heart,' Gisèle said. Her eyes smiled. 'You will find it so, madame.'

When Alex went down to the breakfast table she was carefully cloaked in a cool smile, not sure what reception she would meet, but she found Gaston alone, eating croissants and reading a paper. He jumped up as she appeared, his black eyes flicking over her.

'Good morning.'

Seating herself, she accepted a croissant from the basket he offered and watched as he poured her a cup of delicious coffee, adding a swirl of cream at her assent.

'You look very charming, Alex,' he told her.

She looked up from buttering the croissant. The green eyes inspected his face, as though trying to judge the sincerity of his compliment, then she smiled at him, deciding that he had meant it.

'Thank you, Gaston. Where is everyone else?'

'Philippe, of course, has gone to the factory,' he said, a look of surprise on his face, watching her through his dark lashes.

'Of course,' she said, meeting his glance without a

flicker of awareness, although the reply had surprised her. It would not do to allow him to guess how little she knew of Philippe's life. Did he always leave so early for work?

'Elise is in bed,' Gaston added wryly. 'She has fruit juice and coffee in bed each day. Then she will prepare the household books for you.'

A frown corrugated Alex's brow. 'I'd forgotten that.' It was a terrifying prospect. She could never take over the running of a household like this one, she thought miserably. How typical of Philippe to insist that she should!

Gaston appeared to read her expression. He put a hand across the table and patted her bare arm softly. 'No need to look so alarmed,' he consoled. 'I'm sure you will soon learn to run Sarconne. All you need is a little common sense and a calm approach. I'm certain you have both.'

She smiled gratefully at him. At least he did not seem to be her enemy, even if his wife hated her. She needed every friend she could get.

The black eyes lingered on her face, a curious look in them. 'You have a delightful smile, Alex,' he said softly. 'I envy my brother. That red hair invites speculation.'

Her face glowed and she looked away, her lashes fluttering. He laughed. 'Modesty too! An intriguing combination—modesty and passion. Fire and ice.'

'You shouldn't flirt with me,' she said in an attempt at lightness. 'I'm far too newly married, remember.'

'Shall I come back in a few years' time?' he asked, not quite jokingly. 'Will you be bored with Philippe by then?'

She looked at him quickly, her face shocked. 'That wasn't very nice, Gaston.'

He grimaced. 'I'm sorry. I've been married for five very long years, Alex. I know how soon the gilt fades on the gingerbread.'

'Everyone has ups and downs, I suppose,' she said, uncertain how to reply.

'My marriage has been one long down, then,' he said flatly.

Alex bit her lower lip, her lashes lowered against the smooth flushed cheeks. 'Elise is very beautiful,' she offered uncertainly.

Gaston laughed harshly. 'So are icebergs,' he agreed. 'But any sensible man avoids them as a hazard to shipping.'

She looked at him uneasily, wondering just how much he knew about Elise's past relationship with Philippe. Whatever Gaston knew, he was clearly very unhappy. The bitterness in his voice needed no explanation. Pushing back her chair, she said, 'I must see Elise about these books, I suppose.'

'She'll be in the office,' said Gaston. 'I'll show you the way.'

He ushered her along a corridor and opened a door at the end of it. Elise sat at a desk in the starkly furnished little room, her blonde head bent over a pile of books. She gave Alex a freezing glance, then turned her blue eyes on her husband, contempt and dislike clearly written in them.

'Shouldn't you be at the factory? Philippe will be angry if you are late.'

Gaston gave her a sharp little bow. 'I was on my way,' he said tightly, then turned and went out, slamming the door.

Alex winced. The brief exchange had held such bitter emotions that she was amazed that Elise could look so unconcerned. The other woman leaned back in her modern office chair, her pale hands resting on the desk, her blue eyes coldly slipping over Alex.

Lifting her red-gold head, Alex moved to the chair facing the desk and sat down, quietly meeting that cold, hostile stare.

'We still haven't heard how Philippe met you,' Elise said icily.

'Haven't you?' Alex held her facial muscles under control, her eyes level.

The beautiful, hard mouth twisted. 'A rather sudden romance, wasn't it? How did you pick him up? In a hotel bar?' The insult was unveiled, deliberate.

Alex glanced down at the books. 'You were going to explain to me how Sarconne was run,' she said politely.

There was a tense silence. Elise leaned forward, her hands pressing down on the desk. 'I've no doubt you think you're very clever, but there's something about Philippe you ought to know.'

'If there is, he'll tell me,' Alex interrupted. 'About these books ...' Her green eyes held Elise's angry gaze for a moment, then Elise stood up with an abrupt twist of her curved body.

'Very well,' she said furiously. 'These are the household keys. They're clearly labelled. These are the account books. Don't expect me to do a thing to help you. Find your own way around, if you can. Philippe's vindictive—you'll find that out. He brought you here to punish me and he means to jab the knife right home. Damn him—I don't give a damn. We'll go at the end of the month, don't worry. You can keep Sarconne and Philippe—much good it may do you. The house is a monster, and he's a bastard. I hope you enjoy it as much as you think you will!'

Alex sat listening without expression, her eyes fixed on the bitter face. Elise broke off with a gasp and flung out of the room, slamming the door behind her, but not before Alex had seen the brilliant glaze of tears over those blue eyes, and sensed a wild emotion running beneath that anger.

What a mess, she thought. Obviously, Elise was in love with Philippe, even though she had refused all his overtures—and he, she thought, sickened, must be in love with her, yet he had gone out of his way to hurt and humiliate her by bringing a strange wife to Sarconne. Elise wasn't far out when she called him a vindictive bastard. Cold, calculating, vengeful—the dark master of Sarconne was a man to be avoided.

After a moment she moved around the room, looking at the metal cabinets and shelves, the neat piles of documents and account books. How on earth was she supposed to unravel the secrets of Sarconne alone?

She hesitated, then picked up the telephone and dialled the number of Lélie's room. Lélie had told her yesterday to ring her if she needed help, and there was nobody at Sarconne to whom she would rather go for help.

Five moments later she smiled across the office as Lélie came into the room. The dark eyes held a gentle smile as the older woman greeted her.

'I need your help,' Alex said directly. 'Elise has refused to advise me about the running of the chateau.' She indicated the pile of keys, the household books. 'This is the full extent of the help she has offered.'

'I will be happy to help you,' Lélie said. Her lips grimaced. 'I am not surprised to hear that Elise was difficult. I expected something of the kind.'

Alex felt the shrewd, kindly eyes on her face, but refused to allow herself to meet them. She must not discuss her marriage with anyone, she thought, not even Lélie. It would be disloyal to Philippe.

'I've never done anything like this before,' she said instead. 'I'm afraid I have no experience of a big house.'

'You will soon learn,' said Lélie. 'As Philippe said, you have a choice between sinking and swimming. We must make sure you swim.'

Alex glanced at her uncertainly. 'You have known him for a very long time.' Her tone held a faint question. What sort of man was her husband? she wondered. She knew so little about him. He had been careful to tell her nothing, leaving her to find out for herself the secrets of his life.

Lélie's dark eyes were tender. 'All his life,' she agreed. 'He is not an easy man to know; the strong rarely are. It is the weak who reveal themselves readily. They demand sympathy and support from all quarters. The strong cloak their needs from all eyes.'

Alex's brow wrinkled. Philippe had said something of that to her in England. He had married to conceal the love he felt for Elise ... his pride had made it essential that he hide his feelings from everyone, including perhaps Elise.

What had happened between them in the past? Alex ached to know, but knew she would never ask. Her own pride, her own sense of dignity, came between her desire to know the truth and the two who might tell her. She could not discuss it with Philippe, and she must never allow Elise to speak of it either.

Lélie was watching her thoughtfully. 'Philippe

waited a long time to find a woman with whom he wished to share his life,' she said quietly. 'I am very happy now that he has, Alex.'

Alex blushed, her lower lip trembling. If Lélie knew the truth her pleasure would be dimmed. She smiled at her uncertainly.

'Thank you, Lélie.' Her voice held shy warmth and pleasure. The green eyes glowed with a desire for friendship which she made no effort to conceal. She wanted Lélie to be her friend and her smile said so hopefully.

'Come,' said Lélie. 'First, I will show you over the chateau. We will try all the keys.' Her eyes danced. 'There are hundreds, we will be exhausted by the time we are finished!'

It was a mind-blowing experience, Alex thought, following the thin, upright figure from room to room, admiring and incredulous as the rooms unfolded before her one after the other. She stood in front of family portraits, searching unwarily for hints of Philippe, picking out a hard, sensual mouth here, the glint of grey eyes there, quite unconscious of the fact that Lélie watched her, smiling, as she stared at the strong, dark faces of the Sarconne men.

She stared at delicate, fragile pieces of porcelain from the family factory, not daring to lay a hand on them for fear they broke in her fingers. She gazed, entranced, at the endless views of the woods and fields, burning and bright beneath the arching blue sky.

As she came, dazed, out of the last of the rooms she walked straight into Philippe's tall figure, steadied by his hands on her slender shoulders, and looked up at him, first with vague incredulity, then with a return of memory which brought a deep blush to her face.

Lélie stood back, watching, as the grey eyes glinted down on the soft, pink-washed face. Philippe's mouth curved with amusement. 'Don't I get a good morning kiss?' he asked softly. 'You were sleeping like an angel when I left you this morning. I had to force myself to go to work.'

Alex lifted angry green eyes, but found the movement of her head upward a mistake, because as she looked at him his head swooped and his mouth found her lips in a hard, searching kiss.

She forgot everything, passing once more under the spell of his physical allure, swaying against him helplessly, responding with total abandon, her hands clinging to his shoulders.

He withdrew after a moment and smiled into the dazed, aroused face. 'So Lélie has been showing you Sarconne? Have you been given all the keys?'

'Unless you have a secret chamber, Bluebeard,' she said, her spirit returning.

'Only one for you,' he said softly. 'Shall I lock you up and throw away the key?'

'I wouldn't be at all surprised,' she said, and meant it.

His eyes searched her angry green gaze, then his mouth curved in a derisive smile. 'Coward,' he taunted. 'What do you think I am? Some sort of warlord?'

'Aren't you?' She glared at him. 'Ruthless as hell ... just throwing me into this mess and leaving me to sink or swim!'

Philippe laughed. 'You seem to be swimming perfectly adequately. Why all the fuss?'

Alex changed the subject. 'Lélie has been an angel. I've seen everything except the kitchens.'

'Best not to go down there until after lunch,' he said.

'So we had decided,' she told him, her eyes scornful. He need not think she was incapable of working out for herself that it would throw a spanner into the works for her to invade the kitchens while the staff were working at top speed.

He turned and kissed Lélie. 'Thank you, dear,' he said easily, yet with warmth.

Lélie smiled at them both and slipped away. Philippe looked down at Alex, his eyes on the brilliance of her hair. 'Tired?'

'My legs ache,' she complained. 'So many rooms!'

'Do you ride?' he asked, changing the subject.

She shook her head. 'No.'

'Then tomorrow you must begin to learn,' he said.

'Must I?' Her tone was wry. She knew better already than to argue with him.

He grinned at her, his eyes teasing, and made no answer.

'Tell me about Lélie,' she asked. 'How many children does she have?'

'Just Gisèle,' he said. 'She had two, but one of them died. Her son was killed in the same car crash as her husband, five years ago ... it was a tragedy. The lorry which hit their car was in a terrible state, the brakes useless. It took Lélie years to get over it. She is just pulling out of it now.'

Alex sighed. 'Poor Lélie! I like her very much.'

He smiled deeply. 'That is good.'

She let him lead her down to the Royal Chamber. While he was in the bathroom she sat on the window seat staring out over the countryside, her face shadowed. Philippe watched her from the doorway and his voice made her start.

'Stop daydreaming,' he said curtly.

She turned in surprise and found his brow dark. 'I was waiting for you,' she said reproachfully.

'Get ready quickly,' he said. 'We will be late for lunch.'

Alex wondered why his mood had changed. One moment he had been a teasing, flirtatious husband, the next a dark stranger. Shrugging, she went into the bathroom and washed quickly, before applying fresh make-up.

Elise gave Philippe a sly, sidelong look as they entered the diningroom. Alex pretended not to notice the exchange of glances between them. She sat down, already beginning to be accustomed to taking the head of the table. Her silk napkin slithered to the floor as she unfolded it and Gaston bent to pick it up at the same time as she did, bumping his head against hers. She gave a faint cry of pain, and he exclaimed regretfully.

'I am so sorry, Alex.' He leant forward and kissed her forehead softly. 'There, I've kissed it better.'

She smiled at him unconsciously. 'It was an accident.'

As she turned back to her plate her eyes collided with Philippe's and she was astonished by the angry darkness of his eyes. He looked away, his eyes on his own meal, and she began to eat, wondering why he looked so furious. Surely he could not have objected to Gaston's lightly given caress?

During the meal the conversation was limited and as tense as ever. Alex found herself talking to Gaston most of the time; he was the only one who seemed to want to speak to her. Elise spoke to Philippe from time to time, her tone soft.

After lunch Alex wandered off to find Lélie and together they went down to the kitchens so that Alex might meet the assembled staff. Shyly, nervously, Alex shook hands with them all, while Lélie stood at her shoulder. She sensed a protective impulse in the older woman, and was grateful for it. She accepted a cup of coffee, sat down at the long, scrubbed table and listened while the cook, a short, plump woman in an enveloping apron, talked to her of meals and the price of food. They looked through the kitchen account book together. Alex knew something of catering from her years in hotels. French prices were foreign to her, of course, but she needed no tuition in the problems of catering for a large number of people, and the cook soon saw her experienced understanding and was more friendly. They parted on good terms, and Alex felt sure she would soon get the hang of that part of the management of Sarconne.

'Who runs the other work?' she asked Lélie, and was delighted and unsurprised to discover that Lélie was, in fact, the housekeeper now.

'So you see, it is not so hard as you feared,' said Lélie, smiling. 'We will make it very easy for you, *ma chère.*'

The light endearment was delightful to hear. Alex smiled back warmly at her.

That the running of Sarconne did not merely involve the actual household work alone had not yet occurred to her. She had faced a fence which seemed enormous to her, and taken it without too much trouble. For the moment she was filled with relief.

After dinner that evening she and Gaston played dominoes on a small table in the Salon, giggling as Gaston cheated without mercy. He won three games in a row and she shook her head at him.

'You are unchivalrous,' she accused.

'I like to win,' he shrugged, grinning.

'Only if you deserve to, surely,' she complained.

'I win at all costs,' he said, grimacing.

'Careful,' Elise murmured, looking at them both out of sly blue eyes. 'Philippe may object to such open flirtations, Gaston.'

Alex flushed, turning her bright head towards him. The grey eyes mocked her across the room.

'While they are under my nose, I can afford to ignore them,' he told Elise calmly.

'You're very trusting,' Elise said spitefully. 'Gaston is at home more often than you, remember, Philippe.'

'I know how to guard my own,' Philippe said coolly. 'If Gaston reached out those greedy hands of his to any possession of mine, I would throttle him without a moment's hesitation.'

Gaston laughed oddly. 'Too bad, Elise,' he said ambiguously.

She glared at him and got up. 'I'm tired. I'm going to bed,' she flung, and stalked out.

Later, as she sat in bed watching Philippe wind his watch, Alex pondered on the oddness of that exchange. Gaston and Elise were nothing like husband and wife. Their marriage, she thought, had ground to a halt in the quagmire of distrust and dislike. Poor Gaston! She felt sorry for him.

'Where will Gaston and Elise live when they leave?' she asked Philippe.

He glanced at her sharply. 'At the Dower House.'

'Is that near here?'

'Why?' he asked curtly.

'I just wondered.'

'Afraid you'll miss Gaston when he goes?' he asked.

'His is the only friendly face I see around the meal table,' she retorted, angry with him.

He came over to the bed, his eyes intent. 'Is mine so hostile?' he asked drily.

'I hardly know you,' she said uneasily. 'You're so difficult to get to know.'

He sat down and took hold of her shoulders, shaking her. 'And you are easy?'

'I'm a very simple person,' she said, her eyes wide.

Philippe laughed harshly. 'As transparent as glass,' he said. 'Still dreaming of your worthless young man, Alex?'

Alex flushed. 'I ...' She had barely thought of Hal since last night, she realised. Philippe had filled her head with other ideas, and she found the realisation shameful.

He leant forward, finding her mouth. 'I can put him out of your head for a while,' he said, against her lips. 'Can't I, Alex?'

Shamed, she tried to pull away, but he would not allow it, controlling her effortlessly, his hands compelling, his mouth hard.

'Don't,' she moaned, hating herself for wanting it to go on.

He laughed softly, kissing her throat. 'These helpless little struggles of yours are captivating, didn't you know? They arouse the hunting instinct.'

She shivered. Was that all? She aroused the desire for prey in this predatory male? Her green eyes burned with anger. 'Let me go!'

'You know I have no intention of doing any such thing,' he said mockingly. 'My intentions are perfectly clear to both of us.'

'Philippe,' she groaned before he silenced her, then her head spun in the dazzling, vivid lightning of the emotions he was arousing, her body helpless under the spell of them as he lowered her to the pillows.

She woke very early in a grey dawn light, hearing the deep beat of his heart close to her ear, and turned with a peculiar, trusting delight to snuggle closer to him. For the first time in years she felt at home somewhere, even if it was only an illusion. His arms were a shelter in the darkness, a protection in the alien environment into which he had brought her. He did not love her, she thought sadly, but she was beginning to need him, and she had to admit it. It was not merely his lovemaking which held her. It was a sense of security which his presence gave her.

He moved and looked down at her through half-open lids. She smiled, for the first time, her green eyes melting, and he lowered his mouth to her lips at once, his kiss warm and gentle.

Later, as she and Lélie talked with the cook about the menu for the day, the memory of that kiss came back.

She was unaware that her face had grown soft and tender, her green eyes shining with remembered pleasure. The passion Philippe offered her was a million miles from the exchanged tenderness of that kiss, and it lingered in her mind like a half-remembered melody, haunting and enchanting her.

Lélie and the cook looked at each other, their eyes amused, imagining that they understood.

'So you agree?' Lélie repeated patiently, seeing that she had been unheard.

Alex started, flushing. 'Oh, yes,' she said quickly, having heard not a syllable. 'Yes, of course.'

As the days passed she was beginning to know her way around Sarconne. She had established a routine with Lélie's advice, and as with most routines, it began to seem natural to her as day followed day. She began to look upon the running of the chateau as if she were running a hotel; it made it seem easier. She worked in her office for most of the morning, organising the household, frowning over bills and accounts.

Each morning Gaston rode with her before breakfast—Philippe had suggested it on their first day. Gaston proved to be an excellent teacher. Patient, good-humoured, calm, he soothed away her first fear and encouraged her to relax.

They got on well together. He was kind and cheerful, a gay companion, making her laugh all the time. The slight melancholy she had noticed in him evaporated in her presence, and he never made sly remarks about Philippe again, having seen how they upset her.

Watching him riding beside her one morning, Alex suddenly realised that she felt an odd form of trust towards him, an affection unlike any she had ever known before. He turned his thin face and caught her expression, raising his brows curiously. 'Something wrong?'

Impulsively, she said, 'No, I was just thinking how much I like you.'

Gaston flushed deeply. 'My dear girl!' He laughed sharply. 'Better not let Philippe hear you say that. He might misunderstand.'

She flushed as well. 'I meant ...'

'I think I know what you meant,' said Gaston, smiling, his eyes gentle. 'I feel the same. I never had a sister, but if I had had one, I would have liked her to be like you.'

'Yes,' she said, delighted that he understood. 'I never had any family except my parents, and I always longed for a brother .*.*. now I feel I've got one.'

'You have,' said Gaston, soberly, his eyes very dark. 'You have indeed, Alex.'

'I would trust you with my life,' she said, sighing.

'I would never let you down,' he said at once, then made a wry face. 'This is becoming too intense! Let's see how you can gallop by now.'

They broke into a gallop, laughing at each other, and Alex felt a wild instinctive pleasure in the motion, her red-gold hair flying back from her face, her body moving with her mare, her eyes shining with the pleasure of the exertion. It was, she thought sadly, a pity Elise did not like her. That would always be a barrier.

The hours she and Gaston spent together left an indelible mark which she could not see or comprehend. Anyone seeing them in each other's company would at once become aware of that silent intimacy, that unspoken bond, and Elise's sharp intelligence observed the growth of it with narrowed speculative eyes.

It was not long before she found an opportunity to make Philippe as aware as she was—turning her beautiful, malicious face towards the sight of her husband and his wife as they happily played cards together one evening after dinner, their eyes teasing as they matched wits.

'This time Gaston seems to have completely lost his head,' Elise commented sweetly.

Gaston looked up, the words reaching him, and a dark flush came into his handsome face. Alex lowered her cards, appalled. She looked at Philippe instinctively. He was staring at his brother, his eyes very dark and narrow.

'Bitch,' Gaston snapped fiercely. 'Keep your poison to yourself. And leave Alex alone!'

'Does it hurt to hear her criticised?' Elise mocked.

'I won't even listen,' Gaston ground through his teeth.

'My God, you must be serious about her,' said Elise, not altogether amused.

'Deadly serious,' Gaston said violently. 'So take warning and shut up!'

Elise was white with rage. She looked round at Philippe, her blue eyes inciting him. 'Are you going to sit there and listen while your brother admits he's in love with your wife?'

Alex drew a shaky breath, her hands trembling as the cards dropped from them on to the table.

Gaston glanced at her, seeing her shock, and said tensely, 'Don't put words into my mouth, Elise. I told you to leave Alex alone, that's all. She's no match for a piranha like you and I won't have you trying to attack her.'

Elise laughed, watching Philippe. 'Don't you mind my husband getting so concerned over your wife, Philippe? Or are you sick of her already? You only married her to spite me, we all know that.'

Gaston was on his feet before Philippe could react. Alex watched, horrified, as he slapped Elise so hard that the mark of his rage lay across her lovely face like a burning brand. She gasped in disbelief, her hand flying to her face, but he took her arm, wrenching it behind her back, and hustled her out of the room.

Alex got up in a stumbling, clumsy movement and fled, her body shaken with misery. She could not face

Philippe. She did not have any idea what his reaction to the whole distasteful incident would be. Did he believe the accusation Elise had flung?

She wanted to be alone and silent, to give her mind time to recover its balance.

She made instinctively for the highest, most inaccessible place she knew. There was no sea, no groyne along which she could run into the elements. But there was the donjon catwalk; the high, blinding rush of the wind as it blew across the Limousin and sent the trees spinning like dark tops against the sky.

She leaned on the parapet in the gathering dusk and stared down over the dark green woods, their blown branches hiding the secrets of the hidden depths; the squirrels and birds, the foxes and the long, sleepy green snakes who slept on woodland paths in patches of bright sunlight during the day, gliding away if a human step alarmed them. There was something snake-like about Elise, a sensual love of pleasure, a hiss when she spoke, a dry coldness about her beautiful blue eyes.

Alex's eyes caught the sight of Gaston on his black gelding, riding wildly towards the woods, his thin body graceful on the animal he rode, yet betraying to her by his movements the intensity of his emotions.

Did he still feel something towards Elise? she wondered. They spoke and looked at each other with such barbed hostility, yet they had been married for five years. Surely such a relationship must bind two people together invisibly?

Had their marriage been a happy one until Elise became involved with Philippe?

There were so many questions to which she did not know the answers, and she could not ask anyone anything.

It was obvious to her that whatever had happened between those three in the past it had formed the present at Sarconne, a bitter, troubled present, clouded by twisted emotions. She stared after the disappearing figure of Gaston, sighing.

A movement behind her made her turn, her eyes widening in alarm.

Philippe stood behind her, his body poised tensely. The grey eyes held her glance and she felt her colour rise sharply.

'What are you doing up here?' he asked drily. 'I guessed this was where I would find you when you were not in our chamber.'

She leaned on the parapet, her back to him, making no answer. He joined her, his elbow touching hers, and stared into the sky.

'It is dangerous up here, particularly at this time of the evening. I've told you never to come here alone.'

'I'm not afraid,' she shrugged.

'You are fond of dangerous games,' he said harshly. 'Some are more dangerous than others. Stay away from Gaston, Alex.'

He believed Elise's lies, she thought angrily. She said nothing, and he turned and caught her shoulders, shaking her.

'Did you hear what I said?'

Her green eyes were scornful as she stared back at him. 'Perhaps I should tell you to stay away from Elise, but why should I bother?'

His face froze. 'Why should you, indeed?' he asked tersely. 'You would not be jealous if I were her lover, would you, Alex?'

'Are you?' she asked directly.

'What do you think?' he enquired.

'If you had been, you wouldn't have married me,' she said quietly. 'You told me very plainly why you married me ... to show Elise you didn't love her ... and you succeeded rather too well, it seems, since she's now jealous of me.'

'Jealous of you and Gaston,' he corrected.

She looked at him straightly. 'Elise doesn't love Gaston, we both know that. So does Gaston.'

The grey eyes held her gaze. 'And Gaston has not been in love with Elise for a long time,' he said quietly. 'Now, though, I think Gaston is falling in love again, Alex. So you will promise me to stay away from him.'

'Why should I?' she asked, angry because she guessed he made the demand for Elise's sake.

'You'll do as I request,' he said flatly.

'Will I?' She was not sure at that moment. The temptation to rebel beat in her blood.

'You know you will,' Philippe said coolly.

Alex turned away and stared at the dark woods, wondering what thoughts were going through Gaston's head as he rode there in the breathing woodland paths.

At her back, Philippe said quietly, 'I am sorry if you find it painful, but I must insist.'

'Gaston is my only friend here,' she cried childishly.

'There would be no surer way to lose him than to encourage him,' Philippe told her. 'You can only hurt him. He has borne enough already, Alex.'

She turned at that, her eyes puzzled. He sounded as if he cared about Gaston's unhappiness, as if he were sad for his brother.

Her glance searched his face and he read the enquiry in it, his mouth taut and wry.

'Do you think me completely without feeling?' he asked angrily. 'He's my brother. I've watched for the last five years as he lost heart. You never knew him before his marriage. He was a warm, lively boy once with a great capacity for enjoyment. Five years have eaten it all away and left him like a creature without a soul.'

Alex stared at him, reading his hard, sensual face with disbelief. 'And you can still love her?'

His face closed up as if it were a rock. 'Leave Elise out of this—I am thinking of my brother now. It would be too damnably easy for him to love you, Alex, and I cannot allow it. So give me your word now that it is over.'

'You don't understand,' she cried, searching for the words to explain how she and Gaston were brother and sister, knowing even as she did so that she could never get him to believe it.

'I understand,' he said flatly. 'Elise is not the only one with eyes. From the first, Gaston and you came together like lost children. Now it must stop. He will be leaving the chateau in three days' time. Until then, stay away from him.'

CHAPTER FIVE

DURING the next three days Alex obeyed him and kept away from Gaston, avoiding their usual morning rides, sitting with Philippe after dinner in the evenings. Elise said nothing as she watched Philippe deliberately capturing his wife's attention, but her blue eyes turned again and again, pointedly, towards Gaston. Pale and expressionless, he pretended to read in a chair apart from the others, his face set. Elise said not a word to him, but Alex was as aware of what she did not say as she suspected Gaston and Philippe were ... those icy blue eyes were eloquent and spiteful.

Alex suffered for Gaston, aware that beneath his pretence of calm absorption he was in pain. Once he glanced towards her as he rose to go to bed and their eyes met briefly, leaving her in no doubts as to his feelings. Gaston was unhappy.

Like herself, he had grown accustomed to the relaxed happiness of the time they spent together out of the cold circle of this family which was no family. Elise was a chilling creature to be with, she thought wryly. She froze the blood in one's veins. Gaston's had been frozen for a long time. She was still sure that his affection for her was that of a brother for a sister; there had never once been a romantic moment between them. But who would believe that? Or believe that, in spite of all the evidence, it was this easy warm companionship they both missed, not the passionate love Elise wished to believe Gaston felt for her.

When the day arrived for the move to the Dower House Alex kept discreetly out of the way until Gaston and Elise were leaving. Then she stood in the hall with Philippe at her side, mouthing a polite sentence of good wishes. Elise gave her a spiteful smile.

'I'm sure you'll miss Gaston,' she said, glancing at him with a flick of her lashes. 'Never mind. Think how he'll be eating his heart out for you at the Dower House.' Her laughter had a high, cold derision which made Alex stiffen angrily.

'Why do you say such things?' she asked before she had had time to consider the wisdom of retorting in kind.

The blue eyes were curious. 'Because they are true, my dear,' Elise retorted, her mouth malicious. 'Hasn't he told you yet? Never mind, he will.'

'Get out!' Gaston interrupted curtly, his voice shaking. 'Get out, Elise!'

Elise looked at him and read his implacable hatred. She turned her shoulder, gracefully walking out of the door. 'I'll be seeing you, Philippe,' she said softly as she vanished.

Elise had left the door open. The silvery drops of water played into the scalloped shell in the courtyard. The scent of flowers blew into the chateau on a soft breeze.

There was a silence. Gaston moved slowly towards her, ignoring his brother.

Reluctantly she turned her head, her face brightly flushed with embarrassment, her green eyes sad. '*Adieu*, Gaston,' she whispered.

He stared down into her face as though memorising every feature, the black eyes deeply intent. 'I am sorry all this has happened, *chérie*,' he said huskily. 'Forget it if you can. I hope it has not ruined ...' His voice broke and he half turned away, then halted and faced her, a peculiar smile on his finely shaped mouth.

'*Adieu, chérie,*' he said roughly, bending his dark head. Alex instinctively raised her face at the gesture, expecting him to kiss her cheek, but he turned her head with a hand against her cheek, his mouth finding hers. There was no passion, only sadness in the kiss. Had they been alone she would have burst into tears. The warm, fond relationship between them had been destroyed by Elise. She knew it as well as Gaston did—and it hurt her. She had thought for a little while she had found a brother, a true friend whom she could trust and rely on, and now it lay in shattered fragments around her feet.

Philippe's hand closed like a vice on the soft flesh of her upper arm, pulling her back from Gaston, hurting her so much that she almost gasped with pain.

Gaston gave Philippe a brief unsmiling look, then walked out. The door slammed. The car started. They heard the sound of it rattling over the drawbridge.

'Tell me again that he does not love you,' Philippe said quietly.

Alex looked at him, wondering how he could be so blind. Couldn't he see that Gaston loved her as he would a sister?

'I hope he loves me,' she said, not caring in her hurt how it sounded. 'Because I love him too.'

The grey eyes flared darkly. 'I see,' he said.

'I doubt if you do,' she told him scornfully.

Alone in the chateau, Alex missed Gaston more than she had ever expected. Dining alone with Philippe in the evenings, she ached with loneliness. They seemed to have nothing to say to each other. Each night, as they lay in the great silken bed, she wondered if he would make love to her, and knew that the passion he offered was a physical simulation of love which hurt more than it pleased, although she never tried to deny him. To deny Philippe was to deny herself; she had admitted that now. She needed the caresses he gave her as much as she needed air and light. Silently in the dark room her body flamed in his arms and she responded without barriers, never allowing herself to think because to do so was to open the door to such pain she could not bear it.

Philippe spent hours every day at the factory. Gaston worked there in a subordinate position, but Philippe, as in everything else, was the man in command. Sometimes when Philippe worked late in the evenings, Alex wondered if he was meeting Elise secretly, but his passion as they lay in bed made her convinced that he was not Elise's lover, much as he might like to be, much as Elise might wish it.

She was horrified one evening after dinner when Philippe said casually, 'I think it is time we began to entertain. The whole district has been consumed with curiosity about you, but they have waited for you to settle in at the chateau before they met you. We will have to give some dinner parties.'

Alex was stricken at the idea. 'I couldn't!' she burst out.

'Of course you could,' he said flatly. 'Everything at the chateau is running like clockwork. You've shown how well you can run Sarconne. I told you that you could. I know you better than you know yourself.'

The green eyes glowed for a moment before the long lashes cloaked them. 'Thank you,' she whispered huskily.

He watched her, his eyes on the soft curve of cheek and chin. 'Now you must take up the position of my wife in public, and entertain my friends. You have a position in life to maintain. It's expected of us to move in society.'

'They will all be strangers to me,' she protested nervously, her fingers winding together.

Philippe leaned over and unlaced them firmly, as if the sight of her anxious little movements irritated him. 'You will soon learn to know them,' he said. 'They will be eager to meet you halfway. All you have to do is be yourself and you will win them over easily.'

Alex sighed, admitting defeat. 'Very well, Philippe.' She was absurd even to try to pit her strength against his—he always won in any conflict between them, both in and out of bed. There was never to be a shadow of doubt as to who was master at Sarconne. Philippe brooked no opposition. Had she known him better she would never even have considered marrying him; she would have run like a frightened deer at the first suggestion.

He leaned towards her again, lifting her chin so that her eyes met his. 'Don't look so petrified,' he said wryly. 'Have I ever been wrong before? I told you that you would take to running Sarconne, and you must admit you have. Believe me now. You will like my friends.'

The green eyes widened under his gaze. 'I'll try,' she promised shyly.

His fingers caressed her chin, his eyes watching unreadably as her colour rose beneath her skin.

'By the way,' he said casually, still watching her, 'the first evening we shall have to have Elise and Gaston here. People will be watching to see if we do. There has been some gossip about what happened and it must be quashed at once.'

'Elise is unlikely to make that easy,' she said hardly, her eyes growing angry.

'I'll see to Elise,' he said, his mouth taut.

Her eyes dropped away from his face. 'I'm sure you will,' she said pointedly.

His fingers tightened on her chin, shaking her head slightly. 'Do I need to assure you that I am not Elise's lover?' he asked her tightly.

'No,' she retorted. 'I don't give a damn either way. Elise is not a subject I care to discuss.'

She felt the anger in him. There was a silence, then he asked sharply, 'Is Gaston? Have you seen him since he left?'

'No,' she said bitterly.

'My heart bleeds for you,' he said savagely. 'Is it tragic, Alex, losing another lover so soon after the first?'

Hurt made her reckless. 'I haven't lost Gaston,' she threw back.

'What is that supposed to mean?' Philippe asked in a flinty voice.

'Work it out for yourself,' she told him, walking out of the room without a backward look.

When she saw him later that evening she was tensed for the inevitable conflict which she suspected would break out, but he made no reference to what she had said. She lay in bed nervously watching as he joined her in the darkness. He lay on his side, staring down at the pale oval glimmer of her face, and she hoped he could not hear the wild, fierce beating of her heart.

The dark head bent slowly. His mouth brushed lightly over her lips and her heart beat louder and faster. The hard, possessive mouth returned in the same teasing, elusive fashion again and again until with a muffled cry of hunger she put up her hands to hold his head and draw it down to her.

Then his kiss changed, parting her trembling lips with force and passion, and he began to make love to her hungrily, holding her slender body in his arms as if his desire for her were more than just the physical need she knew it to be, so that, although she could not deny him, she ached with misery as she submitted.

If only, she thought longingly, he would forget Elise, he might in time come to love her. After all, they were together each day, thrown constantly into each other's company. He seemed to enjoy being with her at times. They had at least this physical bond between them, and it was strong—there was no denying that. They had become pleasurable lovers. She might not know the thoughts in that secretive dark head, but she knew very well how to please him when they made love; that much he took no trouble disguising from her. She slid her fingers caressingly down his back and heard, with triumph, the muffled groan he gave as he buried his face against her neck.

Alex was surprised when Philippe suggested that they visit Paris for a weekend before their first dinner party. 'I want you to buy some new evening dresses,' he said. 'You must look as lovely as possible for my friends.'

So that he might not be ashamed of her, she thought bitterly. Or was he still punishing Elise?

They drove to Paris along the fast autoroutes on the Friday evening. It was late when they arrived at their hotel, and she was happy to fall asleep within minutes of getting into bed. She awoke in the morning, puzzled by the faint swish of cars beyond their window, forgetting where she was for a while, wondering vaguely if she was back in the hotel by the sea in England, her past months in France eliminated in that instant of oblivion. For a moment she felt different, a stranger to herself, and then back came Sarconne, Gaston, Elise ... and Philippe ... and she gave a little whimper of pain as memory took over.

'What is it?' Philippe asked, watching her as recollection came into her white face.

She looked at him with empty green eyes. 'Nothing,' she said faintly.

His mouth compressed. 'Gaston?' he said drily. 'Or that selfish young swine in England? I know that look, Alex. You never show that dreamy, sentimental face to me.'

Recklessly she flung back, 'I never will!'

'Thank you,' he said, meaning it. 'I would find such a response boring, to be frank. At least while you are in my arms I hold a woman, not a sentimental adolescent.'

Her face burned. 'Physical response is all you understand, Philippe.'

'It is all I get,' he said coldly.

'Do you want more?' she asked angrily.

'Could I have more?' he retorted.

'You're ruthless,' she muttered, her eyes filled with bitterness. 'You would take everything, if you could.'

'Yes,' he said, staring at her. 'Everything.'

A peculiar vibrant response quivered inside her. She yearned with a terrible desire to give him everything freely, abandon her self-respect, her pride, her whole being. It was the first time she had ever had such a thought. She could not understand herself. Over the weeks of their marriage she had become deeply accustomed to his lovemaking, responding without caring that his desire for her was a physical one. It had been a desire she could understand because it was one she shared. She had ceased to pretend even to herself that she did not want him. He had taught her to need his lovemaking. Suddenly she saw that he had taught her to need him, too, and the pain that thought began ached inside her like an open wound.

What else was this need to give to him if it was not love? A love such as she had never known or recognised before, a wild, painful bitter love which had grown silently inside her until she saw it had taken over her whole being.

Their eyes met and she quivered, glancing away. He must not even guess at her emotions. Philippe was a man without mercy; she knew that from the way he had treated Elise.

She lay back on the pillows, staring at the ceiling. 'We hardly know each other even now,' she said quietly.

'Is that my fault?' he asked, turning on his side to watch her face.

'It's not mine.'

'No? From the start, you turned to my brother rather than to me,' he said flatly.

'Gaston was kind to me.'

'I was not?'

'No, you were ruthless, as always,' she said. 'You take, Philippe. You never give.'

'Then I shall take now,' he said thickly, pulling her towards him, his fingers tangled in her loose hair.

Alex struggled, angry suddenly. It was the first time for weeks that she had attempted to refuse him, and his response was explosive. He jerked her up against his body, his hands violent, and crushed her mouth under his own, burning her lips with the heat of his passion.

She gasped, trembling, and the fight went out of her. What was the point? she asked herself wearily. It was what she wanted. Her arms went round his neck, her body clung helplessly to him as she kissed him back eagerly, her mouth ardent under the demand of his bruising lips.

They made love with a wildness that surpassed every other moment they had spent together, so that she almost fainted with the torture of the sweetness of it.

Later, they spent several hours at an exclusive salon choosing three gowns for her to wear when they entertained. Philippe was tireless in his pursuit of the right clothes. He shook his head over dozens they were shown. Alex made no attempt to argue with him, submitting to his will without protest. It did not escape her attention that several of the models who paraded before them were much struck by the dark, forceful good looks of her cold-eyed husband. They eyed him appreciatively as they strolled languidly up and down. Philippe was indifferent to them, his grey eyes piercing only as they inspected the gowns.

They spent that evening at a theatre, and over supper, late that night, Philippe surprised her by talking more freely than usual. Was it the wine he had drunk? she wondered, listening as he spoke of the factory, the farms, the vineyards. She was impressed by his cool intelligence, his forceful ideas about the future of his business. She wondered briefly if he was trying to show her more of himself, aware of the truth of her accusation that they barely knew each other.

Away from the chateau, she felt rather more free, recovering something of her own personality. Sarconne was so beautiful, so old, so powerful, that she had gradually felt herself being absorbed by it, as if it were a living entity which she could not exist beside in any individual sense. It swallowed whole everyone who came near it. Alex had felt it when she first laid eyes upon it—that monstrous beautiful building waiting in the sunlight for any human life which strayed within its ambience, as if it lived by consuming life.

On the Sunday morning she begged Philippe to take her for a walk beside the Seine before they left for Sarconne. He looked at her thoughtfully before agreeing. They wandered along the banks in the sunlight watching fishermen and artists in the morning light, hearing the slap of water on the sides of moored boats, the ringing of church bells, the whisper of trees from gardens near the river. Alex wore a white dress cut on simple lines which gave her a youthful grace as her slender body swung along beside him, her bright hair glinting in the sunlight. A young man in a blue sweater and jeans stood aside to let them pass, eyeing her with admiration, and she smiled back at him unselfconsciously.

Turning her head, she caught Philippe's grey eyes on her and flushed, suddenly aware of him.

As they drove back to Sarconne she felt a grim reluctance to see it again, afraid of its effect upon her. The months within its walls had changed her; she was deeply aware of that. She had come to it as an unhappy, lost young girl, and had slowly lost her individuality to it. At times she wondered if she existed at all, except as the chatelaine of Sarconne and the woman who shared Philippe's bed at night, and neither of those seemed to have any volition or meaning in her own character.

Lélie welcomed them back smilingly in the court-yard. The sun was sinking slowly, gilding the leaded windows and giving a poignant beauty to the flowers which spilled down the colonnade.

Alex instinctively went into Lélie's arms, as into a mother's, hugging her, kissing her cheek, with an emotion she had never shown her before.

Lélie held her tightly, looked oddly into her green eyes, as if questioning her, although her response was warmly loving.

Philippe took Alex's arm in that tight, possessive grip of his, making her jump, her eyes turning to his face in surprise. His features were set in a cold mask out of which the hard grey eyes stared at her penetratingly, as if filled with hostility. She was puzzled. Why should he object if she kissed Lélie warmly? It was absurd to suspect jealousy. Why on earth should he mind if she showed affection for others?

Next morning Philippe suggested that they ride together before he went to work. She had ridden little since Gaston left. She had had no particular desire to ride alone, and she had been faintly afraid she might meet Gaston as she rode. The Dower House, although it was a mile away, was within easy riding distance, and she had a suspicion that Gaston rode the same woodland paths they had used together.

Alex had never ridden with Philippe before, and she was impressed by his easy, powerful handling of the great rangy bay stallion he kept for his own use. Gaston had told her once that he could not ride Astor. 'He is a one-man horse,' he grimaced. 'Like all Philippe's possessions, he is unique.'

Watching him now, as he rode beside her under the dark canopy of branches, Alex could understand why Gaston had never been tempted to mount Astor.

The power and spirit of the animal were apparent, although under Philippe's cool handling they were never out of control. Astor and his master respected each other, but it was a balance of power between them. Alex suspected that Astor was in spirit unbroken, untamed, a half wild creature of enormous strength who admitted Philippe to his back under loving protest.

When they entered the forest ride which wound up and down over the hillside, they galloped freely. Her red hair flew loose from the confining band she had entrusted it to, and the wind flung it behind her like a silken banner. She found the ride exhilarating. Her green eyes burnt excitedly in her flushed face, and she felt her mouth curving in a smile of delight.

When they returned to Sarconne, Philippe lowered her from her mare, his hands lingering on her waist, and she smiled up at him happily.

He bent and kissed her, his hands sliding her slender body closer. She wound her hands around his neck, thrusting them into the black hair, her neck arched, her body yielding freely to his hands.

Reluctantly he lifted his mouth, and she was aware of the reluctance, delighted by it.

'I must change and go to work,' he said flatly.

'So must I,' she said, her eyes amused.

'Yes,' he said, smiling back. 'We both have duties. I shall not be back for lunch, by the way. I have a board-room luncheon. I will see you tonight at dinner.'

Alex and Lélie spent the day carefully planning the menu for the first dinner party. There were to be eight guests, including Gaston and Elise, and Lélie knew all of them well. She quietly told Alex all she could about them. Two of the men were directors of the factory. Etienne Couvain was in his fifties, Lélie said. His wife was a sharp, clever woman some years younger. They had two children, a son and daughter. Then there was Jacques Lirodin. He was the same age as Philippe, but of a very different character—something of a playboy, Lélie said, grimacing. His wife was a sad creature, very neglected, spending all her time with her four children. 'Madame Lirodin is a doormat,' Lélie sighed. 'If Jacques were my husband I would kick up a fuss, I can tell you, but she sighs and acts the martyr and it goes on ...' She gave Alex a brief look. 'Elise and Jacques were once very friendly, but it ended a year ago.'

A year ago, thought Alex. Was that when Elise turned her attention to Philippe?

Aloud, she asked, 'And the last couple?'

Lélie smiled. 'They are younger ... they live three miles from here. Marie and Pierre have three children. Pierre works one of the Sarconne farms. He is a good, modern farmer and he has improved the farm beyond recognition. Philippe likes to encourage him. He has helped him to buy a lot of modern farm machinery, to modernise the farm buildings. It helps them both. Pierre is an excellent tenant, so Philippe is an excellent landlord.'

Philippe added some comments of his own later, telling Alex that he wanted her to make friends with the three wives. 'Marie St Georges will be just the woman to help you with local society,' he added. 'She enters into things wholeheartedly. Everyone knows her and likes her. I would like you to be friendly with her.'

'And the husbands?' Alex asked. 'Which of them am
I to make friends with?'

He gave her a cool look. 'Is that intended as a joke?'
She flushed. 'If you like.'

'Not Jacques,' he said curtly. 'The others you may
charm if you wish, but Jacques is dangerous.'

She saw what he meant as soon as she met Jacques
Lirodin. He was a lean, elegant man with a sensual face
and bright, impudent blue eyes. As he bent to kiss her
hand she felt the shock of his long glance over her
body as if it were a direct assault, and flushed.

'What an enchanting dress,' he said, and the slight
hesitation before the last word made it an ambiguous
compliment.

'It's charming,' Marie St Georges said quickly, stepping forward to take Alex's hands in her own.

Alex smiled easily at her, liking her at once. A slim,
capable young woman a little older than herself, with
streaked brown hair and brown eyes, Marie was open
and friendly.

The Salon which had seemed on so many evenings to
be a silent shrine was suddenly filled with people and
voices. In her finely pleated grey dress, the colour
shading from something approaching black to a pale
ivory, the silk clinging where it touched, outlining her
slender breasts and hips, Alex moved from one to
another like a drift of silken smoke, smiling and talking politely. The colour softened her vibrant hair to a
warm glitter and made her green eyes seem brighter
and more vivacious.

The dreaded meeting between herself and Gaston
and Elise had passed off without incident. Elise, in an
ice-blue gown, seemed quiet and reserved. Gaston was

drawn and haggard in his black clothes, his eyes like a flame in the pallor of his face.

Over dinner Alex talked to Pierre St Georges with great pleasure, finding him an easy companion. When she turned to Madeleine Lirodin she anticipated a difficulty which she found did not exist. Madeleine was eager to talk to her and Alex listened politely while the other woman chattered of her children, her home, her husband, barely taking breath to ask any questions or seem aware of anything but her own concerns. It was, Alex found, a comforting conversation. The frictions around the table, of which she was deeply aware, seemed not to exist for Madeleine.

The meal was a triumph. Lélie, the cook and Alex had planned it meticulously, and nothing had gone wrong. Everyone was filled with compliments, and Philippe had a satisfied expression as they left the table. His hand slid under Alex's elbow, his grey eyes smiled at her without reservation.

Marie St Georges nervously asked her, in the Salon, if it might be possible for her to see some of the great art treasures of Sarconne. 'I so rarely get a chance to see any art,' she sighed. 'The farm is too demanding— not to mention the children.'

Alex was delighted to take her round the long gallery which ran the length of the house on the first floor, the walls lined with family portraits, although not all of them were of any particular merit. Their age conferred charm upon them, anyway, in her opinion, and Marie clearly shared her view.

Alex was disturbed to find that Jacques Lirodin had followed them up to the gallery. He wandered along behind them, his hands in his pockets, his unscrupulous blue eyes upon Alex's figure as she walked beside

Marie. The warm weather had broken that day, and rain began to spatter upon the leaded panes of the gallery as they walked back to the stairs. Just as Alex was following Marie down to the Salon, Jacques asked casually, 'Is this a genuine Fragonard, or a copy?'

She turned and saw his eyes upon a charming rural scene, a picture tucked away in a corner, with a pretty, rosy-cheeked girl in a yellow silk dress swinging from a beautifully painted elm.

Reluctantly she paused. 'No,' she said. 'It's a copy, I believe.' That, Philippe had said, was why it was in a corner in the darker part of the room.

Jacques moved closer to it. 'It looks genuine enough,' he commented.

Alex had to return, out of sheer courtesy, to stand beside him and eye the painting without real interest.

'She's almost edible,' he murmured softly. 'Nearly as sexy as you, Alex.'

She backed too late. He had swung, smiling mockingly, and was reaching for her, his hands grasping her hips in a movement which sent a wave of angry distaste through her.

'Let me go!' she exclaimed furiously.

'Oh, come on, sweetheart,' he said thickly. 'Philippe won't miss one kiss, and I've had nothing else on my mind since I saw you.'

Alex swung a clenched fist at him, aiming for his smiling, selfish face, suddenly seeing Hal and filled with a hatred for all men. Did they all take what they wanted without compunction?

The smile vanished and Jacques's eyes grew ugly with thwarted desire and wounded vanity. He began to pull her towards him, his hands hurting, ignoring her angry struggles and flashing eyes.

The next moment Alex was free, flung away ungently. Even as she took in Gaston's presence, Jacques was measuring his length upon the polished wooden boards of the gallery and Gaston stood over him, his fists clenched bitterly.

'Get up and I'll knock you down again,' he spat. 'I can't wait to push that lascivious smile of yours down your throat, you swine!'

'No, Gaston,' Alex protested anxiously, moving to put a hand on his arm, feeling the bitter tension of his muscles under her touch. 'Forget it. This is a party. Don't spoil it.'

Slowly, reluctantly, he turned his head. The dark eyes were filled with fire. Alex looked pleadingly into them, and saw a wild consciousness return, as if for a moment he had forgotten where he was.

'I am sorry, *chérie*,' he said deeply. 'I lost my temper. That devil deserved it.'

Jacques got up, ostentatiously dusting off his dark trousers and walked away. As he vanished he said spitefully, 'I'll leave you in Gaston's hands, then, Alex. I see you would prefer his hands to mine.'

She felt her cheeks burn at the remark, and Gaston turned, his eyes flaming, but Jacques had hurriedly removed himself, and she caught at Gaston's shoulder to detain him, afraid of what he might do if he caught up with the other man.

Gaston breathed deeply, his mouth taut, his eyes on the floor. Alex watched him anxiously, aware suddenly that he was quite clearly at the end of his tether. Since she last saw him he had suffered appallingly somehow. He looked quite ill.

'Are you all right, Gaston?' she asked in a worried voice.

He turned his dark head to look at her, and a
peculiar quiver ran over his thin face, 'No,' he said
huskily. 'How can I be, shut out from paradise?'

The reply puzzled her. Then she said, sighing,
'Sarconne, you mean? Oh, I am sorry, Gaston. I regret
being the cause of you leaving your home.'

'I do not,' he said oddly. 'Had you never come to
Sarconne I would never have met you, and even hell
can seem sweeter than emptiness, Alex.'

She stared, her brow creased, concentrating on him,
completely unaware of the man who had just entered
the gallery from the stairs.

'Gaston?' her voice faltered.

'Oh, Alex,' he breathed thickly. 'Alex, my sweet ...'

She had no time to back, to think, to put a distance
between them. His arms came round her and he took
her mouth with a hunger she could feel through every
inch of her body, a hunger which burned and begged,
terrifying and alarming her, making her shudder with
compassion and incredulity.

For one moment she stood, feeling the kiss intensely,
then she put her hands on his shoulders and pushed at
him frantically. 'No!' she half sobbed against his
pleading mouth.

He held her shoulders, staring down into her white
face.

'Gaston, please,' she whispered. 'I'm your brother's
wife ...'

'That never stopped him,' he said bitterly.

Her eyes registered the blow. 'Don't,' she said in
pain.

'No,' said a cool, noncommittal voice behind them
both. 'Don't, Gaston ... it was clearly a mistake to invite you here. I think you and Elise should leave now.'

Gaston released her and turned to face Philippe. White-faced and distraught, Alex looked past him at her husband.

She could sense Gaston's jealousy, passion and violence growing inside him with every second and she was terrified of the explosive nature of the emotions consuming him. Her head seemed to be swimming wildly, as though thought were becoming impossible, only feeling having any reality, and the feelings which were swamping her were nameless. She swayed, a hand to her head, the bright red-gold hair seeming too heavy for her to carry. Gaston turned abruptly, sensing her weakness, and caught her in his arms as she slumped senseless.

'Alex,' he groaned in anguish, holding her close to his body, her bright head on his dark shoulders like a flower. 'My darling!'

Philippe removed her silently, grimly, from his brother's arms. His grey eyes surveyed Gaston with pity and command. 'Take Elise and go home, Gaston,' he said, his voice flat. 'I will look after my wife.'

He rang for Lélie when he reached their chamber. Alex was stirring, her face whiter than paper, her green eyes enormous between their heavy lids.

'Look after her,' Philippe commanded briefly. 'I must look after our guests.'

Left alone with Lélie, Alex burst into tears and clung to her as she cuddled her comfortingly. 'The dinner party has been ruined,' she sobbed. 'What could I do? That awful man!'

'Which one?' Lélie asked humorously.

Alex gave her a brief account of what had happened. 'He's quite revolting,' she said, shuddering. 'What Elise could see in him when she was married to Gaston!'

Lélie looked down curiously upon her bright head.
'Love is a strange virus. It strikes where one does not
expect it and vanishes before one has a chance to
understand it.'

Alex stared at the gilded splendour of her silken
room. 'Poor Gaston,' she sighed sombrely. 'Poor
Gaston!'

CHAPTER SIX

To Alex's great relief Philippe seemed unwilling to discuss the incident. She was asleep when he came to bed that night, and next morning he had gone when she woke up, so that she spent the day in nervous expectation of their meeting later, but when he returned for dinner he behaved as though nothing out of the ordinary had occurred during the dinner party, his face calm and unreadable.

They talked during the meal, their voices coolly polite, while the servants moved discreetly around behind them. Philippe talked about the factory, made a few satisfied comments on the quality of the grapes this year, prophesying a good year, a good vintage. Alex sighed over the cost of some material she had bought to make new curtains for some of the bedrooms. It was to be made up by herself and Lélie, but Philippe frowned over that.

'Get a seamstress,' he said curtly. 'You have enough to do.'

'I like to be busy,' she said, her tone faintly depressed.

The grey eyes shot to her face, narrowing. He said no more, but his mouth compressed.

After dinner they sat in the Salon, listening to music, the dazzling cascade of Debussy reminding her of the fountain playing in the courtyard on a summer day. She leaned back in her chair, her eyes dreamy, and Philippe watched her through half closed lids.

'What are you thinking about?' he asked tersely.

'You have that look on your face again.'

She looked at him, startled. 'I was thinking about the fountain in the courtyard. Doesn't this sound like it?'

His brow rose sharply. He made no answer, staring at her as if probing behind her calm, serene expression. At times lately, she thought, there was a volcanic impatience about him, as if he were poised on the brink of some enormous explosion. Was he finding the strain of their marriage as unbearable as she was? Or did his passion for Elise drive him day and night?

'Shall we ride tomorrow morning?' he asked. 'I have no urgent appointments until eleven.'

'That would be nice,' she agreed, smiling at him in her pleasure, the green eyes glowing.

He leaned back, the grey eyes oddly dark, staring at the glowing colours of the painted ceiling, as if the half-clothed, roseate shapes of the women fascinated him. 'Are you beginning to settle in at Sarconne, Alex?' he asked without looking at her. 'You seem to be part of the household already.'

'Lélie and the others have made me feel at home,' she said evasively.

'Haven't I?' he asked wryly. The hard profile tightened in anger.

'You've been very kind,' she said nervously.

'Kind!' His mouth twisted. 'What do you know of passion, Alex? Only what I have taught you, and even then you aren't sufficiently adult to finish the equation, are you?'

She groped for his meaning, her eyes anxious. 'What do you mean?'

His expression gave her no clue. 'Nothing. Forget it,' he muttered. He patted the silken sofa on which he was lounging. 'Come and sit with me. Why do you always sit so far away? The only time you come close to me is in our bed, and delightful though that is, it is hardly sufficient for a good marriage.'

Flushed, Alex rose and joined him, sitting down nervously, a foot away from him. He reached out a strong hand and jerked her nearer, looking down into the nervous green eyes penetratingly.

'That's better,' he said drily. 'Now, tell me what you thought of Marie St Georges and her husband.'

'I liked them both. Marie has invited us back to their house, by the way. She rang this morning to thank me for the dinner, and asked if we would go to their house one night soon. I said I would ask when you were free.'

'You would like to go?'

'Very much,' she agreed.

'Good. Thursday would be ideal—I can get the afternoon free. We could ride together before we change for dinner at the farm.'

'Marie has said she'll invite some of their friends so that I can meet a few more local people,' she said huskily, aware in every nerve that he was still holding her hand.

'Excellent,' said Philippe, his long fingers sliding over the invisible veins in her slender wrist, sending a flutter of excitement along her pulses.

'I'll ring her tomorrow and let her know,' Alex murmured, hoping he was not conscious of the way her pulse was leaping.

The grey eyes searched her averted face. 'And what did you think of Jacques Lirodin?'

Bright red colour swept up to her hairline as the question took her by surprise. She gave him a quick, upward look, her green eyes becoming enormous. 'I

detested him,' she stammered. 'I'm sorry if he's a friend
of yours, but I hated him.'

Philippe's mouth moved in a dry smile. 'From what
Gaston said to me just before he left, I gather Lirodin
followed you up to the gallery to make a pass at you?'

She nodded, biting her lower lip. 'It came out of
the blue,' she said in a low voice. 'He's so conceited
that he apparently expected me to fall into his arms ...'

The grey eyes skimmed her face. 'Gaston said he
walked in and found you trying to fight Lirodin off.'

She nodded. 'Gaston knocked him down,' she whispered.

'Chivalrous Gaston,' Philippe drawled.

She gave him a furious look, reading the sarcasm. 'I
was very relieved to see him. That vile man was much
too strong for me. I was on the point of screaming the
place down when Gaston came and stopped him, and
I've never been so pleased to see anyone in my life.'

'And Gaston followed up his gallantry with a pass
of his own,' Philippe said derisively.

Alex's mouth quivered. She had been expecting some
comment, and here it was. Almost pleadingly, she told
him, 'I wasn't expecting it. I was shattered. Gaston had
never done such a thing before. I'm sure it was just an
impulse.'

'You have a peculiar blindness when it comes to
men,' he said drily. 'You seem incapable of reading
their motives. That fiancé of yours pulled the wool
over your eyes successfully for months. Only an act of
fate showed you the truth about him. You're too trusting, too naïve. I did warn you about Gaston.'

'I know,' she said. 'But I thought ...' She was about
to explain that she had genuinely thought of Gaston as
a brother, but the words shrivelled on her lips under

the derisive, mocking grey eyes. Philippe already regarded her as an idiot.

'What did you think?' he asked coolly, watching her changing expressions closely. 'Surely a woman knows when a man is in love with her? Doesn't some instinct warn about such things?'

She shook her head, her eyes sad. 'I had no suspicion,' she said wearily.

'Gaston was hardly difficult to read,' he went on, the grey eyes narrowed. 'He gave himself away a hundred times. And you still pretend you saw nothing?'

'I'm not pretending!'

He shrugged. 'Poor Gaston, he should have made himself clearer a long time ago. Tell me, how did you feel when you realised at last that he was in love with you?'

Alex bent her head, her cheeks heated. 'Please!'

'As your husband, surely I have a right to ask?' he said coldly. 'You very dutifully begged him to remember you were his brother's wife, but before that he kissed you and you did not struggle.'

'I was too shocked and surprised,' she explained. 'Gaston has never given me any reason to suspect ...'

'Elise saw it weeks ago,' Philippe said between hard lips.

She sat up straight, pulling her hand out of his. 'Elise! Oh, do you think I would take her word for anything? She wanted to believe it. She wanted to sow trouble between us, didn't she?'

He stared at her. 'You hate Elise, don't you?'

'She hates me,' Alex said. 'Don't pretend you don't know why—she made it very obvious. How much was there between you two before you married me, Philippe? Gaston seems to think ...'

'Gaston is a fool,' he said flatly. 'If she were my wife, I would have put a stop to her antics years ago.'

'A pity she wasn't, then,' Alex said jealously.

He laughed suddenly. 'How green your eyes are suddenly.' His glance teased lightly. 'Is it possible you're jealous, Alex?'

'Of you? Never,' she said, not meaning a word of it.

'Never?' He pinned her against the silken cushions, his hands possessive, and stared down into her flushed face with grey eyes which taunted. 'Don't be too sure, Alex,' he whispered as his mouth moved down to claim hers.

She lay passive for a few seconds, trying to fight the pleasure the touch of his lips gave her, then she felt a wave of excitement sweep over her as the kiss deepened, and her body relaxed against him, her mouth ardently returning the kiss.

'Our one sure line of communication,' he muttered unsteadily as he withdrew. 'Words are such uncertain instruments, Alex, but we always have one method of getting through to each other, don't we?'

She lay where he had left her, the green eyes drowsy with warm pleasure, the pink mouth slightly parted, swollen with passion.

'Philippe,' she whispered shakily, her eyes pleading.

He stared at her, reading the aroused face in a searching glance, then bent and picked her up into his arms and carried her out of the Salon to their bedroom, kicking the door shut with his foot before he carried her to the bed.

There were no further words between them that night, but the communications, Alex thought dazedly as she responded to his passion, were excellent. She laughed at the thought, her head thrown back as he kissed her throat, and Philippe froze, looking down at her in the darkness.

'Why are you laughing?' There was grimness in his voice.

'Our lines of communication ...' she murmured, her mouth soft.

The grimness went out of his face. He tangled a hand in her red-gold hair, jerking her face up towards him. 'Siren,' he muttered huskily, beginning to kiss her hotly.

She woke at dawn in his arms, stretching lazily, aware of a sensation of wellbeing, a physical radiance which she had never felt before.

Philippe awoke slowly, turning his head to find her, grey eyes soft with amusement as she stretched again, deliberately, enjoying the feel of his body against her as her limbs moved.

'Hurry up,' she said lightly. 'I thought we were going to ride this morning.'

They rode in the autumnal woods, watching the wind catch leaf after leaf and whirl it away into the darkness of the interior. A squirrel ran across their path and shot up a tree, tail quivering. The vivid hues of the branches flowed into each other, red into brown, orange into yellow, the distant vista a glorious multi-hued warmth of mingled shades. Philippe talked of his family's history, making Alex laugh with tales of past escapades and indiscretions. She was beginning to recognise some of the names. Often she and Lélie walked around Sarconne while Lélie sketched in the backgrounds of some of the more notable members of the family.

'My family history is a blank,' she said with amusement. 'My parents were respectable and colourless, like me.'

'Colourless?' Philippe's brows rose and he laughed. 'Is that your honest opinion of yourself?'

She looked at him in bewilderment. 'Compared with your family, yes.'

He moved his mount closer, his knee against hers, and put a hand to her vibrant hair. 'You are a flame, *chérie*,' he said, his voice deep. 'From the first moment I saw you on the beach in England, I couldn't take my eyes off you.'

Her colour rose. 'My hair, you mean?'

'Your hair?' He smiled. 'That was part of it, but it was your spirit that I meant ... your vitality. You ran along that groyne like a flame in the wind, daring the elements with laughter.'

Alex was confused under the grey eyes, her glance falling. There was the sound of hoofbeats among the trees suddenly, and the next moment Gaston rode into sight, his lean body casual in a black sweater and biscuit-coloured breeches. He drew rein, seeing them, and for a few seconds there was total silence as his black eyes took in the intimacy with which Philippe's knee nudged Alex's, his hand curving around her bright head. Alex stared at Gaston, her eyes enormous, remembering the last time they met with stricken embarrassment.

After a moment Gaston turned and rode away without a word or sign of having recognised them, and she let out a long sigh of distress.

Philippe was watching her intently. She turned her mount in silence, acutely aware of him, and rode back towards Sarconne with a heart filled with sadness. She had come between the two brothers without ever having intended it, and she had no idea what to do.

On the following Thursday she and Philippe rode together again, in the warm autumn afternoon, talking of the St Georges farm and the improvements that had been made to it. Pierre was a good tenant, Philippe told her.

'I wish the others were as go-ahead, but they are older and these things take time. Since the Common Market started, French agriculture has made enormous strides, but we still have a long way to go before we are totally modernised. Modernisation takes money. It also takes a certain attitude of mind, a willingness to change with the times, and some of the older tenants refuse to face up to the changes.'

Alex listened seriously, nodding. She liked to hear him talk about the estate. It gave them common ground on which to meet. He might say that their time in bed together was sufficient, but she knew that if their marriage was to work they needed more than that.

'I would like to visit the factory one day and see how it all works,' she told him.

He looked at her sideways, his frown appearing. 'Why?' he asked curtly.

She was puzzled by his hostile face. 'It's where you work. I'm interested.'

'And you might see Gaston,' he drawled.

Alex flushed. 'That was never in my mind,' she said furiously. 'If I wanted to see Gaston it would be simple enough without going to such lengths.'

'Oh?' He watched her soberly. 'Tell me, would you invite him to meet you on one of your morning rides?'

'If I wanted to do so obviously I could,' she said. 'But I don't want to ...'

'Have you ever met him while you were riding?' he

asked casually. 'It was odd the way we ran into him the other morning.'

She flushed. 'It was the first time I'd seen him while I was riding. I rarely go far from Sarconne when I'm alone.'

'It would be wisest to keep it that way,' he said coolly. 'Gaston is a little out of his mind at the moment. Keep away from him, Alex. For his sake.'

She was filled with that sadness which came over her when she thought of Gaston. 'You don't need to warn me,' she said huskily.

'I warned you once before and you took no notice,' he said. 'You remember what came of that.'

'Why doesn't he divorce Elise and start again?' she asked him furiously. 'He's so unhappy.'

'He is a grown man,' Philippe said flatly. 'Leave him to work out his own problems.'

'Poor Gaston,' she said, sighing.

'That is the root of the trouble,' Philippe said coldly. 'You showed him too much sympathy from the start, and after years of being frozen out by Elise, he went mad over you, like a starving man offered the food he craves for.'

Alex flushed deeply. 'Who could help being sorry for him? With a wife like that! Gaston should get away from her, right away.'

'Right away from Sarconne,' Philippe said tautly. 'Away from you ... do you honestly think he would go now? While he has a chance of seeing you, even at a distance, now and then? Do you think I didn't see the way he looked at you the other morning? The poor idiot almost ate you with those miserable eyes of his. I hardly know whether to feel sorry for him or angry with him.'

'It isn't my fault,' she said unhappily. 'I had no idea ...'

'You don't need to tell me that,' Philippe muttered, his eyes sardonic. 'Where your own attraction is concerned, you're as blind as a mole. It should have occurred to me at once, but it took a few days before I realised that putting a warm-blooded, smiling female into Gaston's path was a fatal mistake. He made straight for you as if you were a fire on a cold night.'

Her eyes widened and she turned her head to look at him in involuntary pleasure at the imagery. The grey eyes were fixed on her and as she turned their eyes met.

Philippe stared unsmilingly at her. 'Why look so surprised? Don't you know by now the effect you have on men? Beauty is only skin deep. Elise is beautiful, but she's as cold as northern nights. You blaze on the air, as tempting as sunlight, and I am not just talking about that wonderful hair of yours ... Gaston fell for the warmth in your eyes, Alex, not your hair.'

'What did you fall for in Elise? Her coldness?' Alex asked him bitterly, then turned her horse and rode back towards Sarconne, thinking that she was not the only one around here who was blind. Philippe clearly saw Elise in some other light than the one in which he spoke openly of her—could a man who was in love speak so sharply of a woman? Yet he had not denied that it was Elise he loved, although he had never admitted it either.

That evening she wore a classical white dress for dinner with the St Georges couple. Sleeveless, its silken bodice clung to her body, outlining the rise of her high breasts before it curved in to her waist and out to her slim hips, falling in a sweep to her feet. It had a Grecian purity which the flame of her hair emphasised.

Philippe eyed her slowly as she joined him and she felt her colour rise under the grey gaze.

'Enchanting,' he said sombrely. 'Just as well Gaston is not to see you in it.'

'Stop talking about Gaston!' she flared irritably.

'Gladly,' he drawled. 'If you stop thinking of him.'

'I don't,' she retorted.

'No?' The dark brows arched incredulously.

She looked at him angrily. 'I could almost believe you want me to fall in love with him!'

His eyes narrowed. 'Is that what you tell yourself?'

'Why do you keep bringing him up?' she flung back.

'Perhaps it annoys me that you should have so much warmth and sympathy for others and none for me,' he said coolly.

Alex flushed deeply, turning away. 'Are you ready? We mustn't be late.'

The evening was a friendly, pleasant occasion. There were four other guests beside themselves, all of them in their thirties, two married couples who obviously knew both Philippe and the St Georges very well. They made Alex feel welcome, and under the influence of their friendliness she expanded like a sun-encouraged flower, smiling, talking easily, her natural character coming out from behind the nervous tension of the past weeks.

They talked of books, music, films, their talk flowing easily between them. Freed from the pressures of hostile eyes, of the heavy responsibilities of Sarconne, Alex laughed as she listened to a discussion about Woody Allen and a delighted discussion of cartoon films.

The evening seemed to fly. When she and Philippe left she felt as if she walked on air, her thoughts heady.

'Do we have to drive straight home?' she asked Philippe, leaning back in her seat with a sigh of enjoyment. 'It's such a lovely night. Can't we go for a drive for a little while?'

He glanced at her. 'Why not? The woods look lovely in the moonlight.'

They drove along narrow, winding lanes between the magical woods, watching as moonlight drifted in white clouds through the dark lines of trees, illuminating the secret woodland pools which lay beneath the branches now and then, turning the clustering reeds into silver spears.

Philippe stopped the car slowly and glanced at her. 'Are your shoes up to a short stroll through the trees?'

She looked doubtfully at the delicate white sandals she wore. 'We could try,' she said lightly.

He helped her out with a hand under her elbow and they wandered into the pressing belt of trees, following a sandy path which led beside one of the little pools. Alex stopped to stare across the moonlit water. It had the silken gloss of black leather where the moon did not penetrate, a dense darkness which resisted the eye.

'You were very gay tonight,' he murmured, his eyes on the dark woods.

'I liked everyone I met,' she said frankly. 'They were all friendly and charming, and I felt I had something in common with them all.'

'Are you unhappy at Sarconne, Alex?' he asked abruptly.

She took a deep breath. After a moment, she said huskily, 'Not as unhappy as I was.'

He was silent for a moment. 'It will work out, Alex,' he said quietly. 'Give it time.'

She felt a strange, painful emotion around her heart.

It was quite impossible to answer him. She wanted very much to believe what he said. They were married. It worked out well in bed. She knew by now that she aroused him as much as he aroused her. They got on well together in a slightly tense fashion—enough, she thought, to make it possible that they might one day be perfectly happy together. But Philippe left one thing out of his calculations.

'No answer?' he asked coolly.

Alex sighed. 'I would like to believe it, Philippe. We're married now. Time is something we shall have plenty of.'

'But?' he asked curtly, his eyes on the moonlit water.

'There's love,' she whispered anxiously.

He gave a short laugh. 'Oh, yes, the heart has its reasons, which reason knows not ... following your heart has never done you much good in the past, has it, Alex? First that selfish swine in England, then Gaston ...'

'Please, don't mention Gaston again,' she cried angrily. 'I made a fool of myself over Hal. That's enough.'

'More than enough, I'd say,' he muttered harshly.

She turned back towards the car, moving quickly. But the delicate white shoes were not intended for such rough work. The strap of one snapped as she walked over the uneven ground, and she stumbled.

'What's wrong now?' Philippe asked irritably, reaching her side with a terse movement.

'These shoes were meant for drawingrooms, not woodlands,' she said ironically, supporting herself against him.

He lifted her into his arms and her hands clung to his wide shoulders, the moonlight falling in a silver shower over her uplifted face, turning the flame of her hair to a silvered gleam.

Philippe held her, staring into her face for a moment, then he turned and carried her back to the car and deposited her ungently on the seat beside him.

As they drove down the wide white road to Sarconne, the moonlight fell over it in a shimmering cloak, giving it a mysterious, magical beauty which it had never worn before, and Alex felt a strange delight in seeing it.

'It looks like a fairy castle tonight,' she murmured under her breath.

Philippe glanced sidelong at her, his eyes searching her rapt, moonlit face.

'Can it be possible that you are beginning to love Sarconne?' he asked sardonically.

She flushed. 'It still frightens me, but it's so beautiful.'

'There's hope for us yet, then,' he said ambiguously.

CHAPTER SEVEN

THE autumn drew on in a warm haze, each day beginning and ending with opalescent mists drawn up from the surrounding woods and fields, dispersed as the sun rose higher in the blue skies. The trees were still shedding their leaves slowly, the woodlands thick with heaps of Technicolor brightness which rustled as the horses picked their way along the paths. Some mornings Alex rode with Philippe and others she rode alone, although when he was not with her she rarely went far from the security of Sarconne's strong walls.

Her feelings towards the beautiful building were changing day by day as she grew more accustomed to it. She was spending more and more time in social engagements. She found that as Philippe's wife she was expected to see and be seen on many occasions, and although some of these bored her, at others she found herself surrounded with a friendly, cheerful crowd of companions who accepted her easily as herself, and, by doing so, freed her from the oppressive feeling of being an intruder in this alien world.

She gave several more dinner parties, finding them less and less a strain as time went on, and, without realising it, blossoming under the influence of being part of this new world. Her friendship with Marie St Georges was an important part of her new enjoyment. She and Marie shopped together, rang each other up, gossiped and giggled together.

Alex first realised that she was pregnant one morning

after a dinner party at Marie's house. Philippe had gone to work when she woke up feeling nauseated. She staggered to the bathroom, thinking that it was something she had eaten the night before, and wondering if it could be the result of eating shellfish. Feeling wan and limp, she fell back into bed and lay there, shivering. Only then did her brain connect other symptoms, and a wave of scarlet rushed up her face. How could she have been so stupid as to ignore the possibility? Or had she hoped against hope that she was wrong?

There was little doubt in her mind when the next morning began in a very similar way. She was grateful that Philippe was very busy at the factory at that moment. She was reluctant for him to know, although it was a foolish attitude to take. Sooner or later he would notice, she told herself, but she still could not bring herself to mention it to him; it embarrassed her too much.

She rode that morning, her mind so preoccupied with the fact of her pregnancy that she went further than usual and found herself in the autumnal woods. About to turn and make her way back to Sarconne, she was brought face to face with Gaston.

They stared at each other, immobile, for a long moment.

Gaston slowly edged his horse nearer, his black eyes on her face. Alex flinched from the emotion she too easily read in his handsome, gaunt face.

'Alex,' he muttered hoarsely.

'Hallo, Gaston,' she said, not having an idea how to deal with the situation.

His eyes ran over her face again. 'You look very pale,' he said, his voice deep. 'Are you unhappy?'

She was shaken by the wildness of the hope in his

voice and her eyes widened.

He saw the startled, anxious look come into her face and put a hand suddenly over hers, moving even closer. 'Don't look so frightened, my darling,' he said huskily. 'I wouldn't harm a hair on your head. Don't you know that?'

'Please, Gaston,' she said weakly, withdrawing her hand. 'I must go.'

'Not for a moment,' he said, seizing her reins. 'Just stay for a moment. I haven't seen you for weeks.'

'Well—yes,' said Alex evasively. 'How is Elise?' It was difficult for her to say that name without revealing her hatred for the other woman.

'Elise is in Paris,' Gaston said flatly.

Alex looked at him, the news delighting her. 'Oh?' At least Elise was away from Philippe for the moment, she thought.

'She was bored out of her wits at the Dower House,' Gaston said with a wry twist of his handsome mouth. 'So she took off for Paris to find some amusement there.'

Alex sighed again. 'I'm sorry, Gaston.'

'I don't give a damn,' he shrugged. 'She could vanish off the face of the earth tomorrow and I wouldn't care for a second.'

'Why don't you divorce her?' Alex asked him impulsively. 'It's not a real marriage, is it? Why go on with it?'

Gaston stared at her, his black eyes flaming. 'Would you divorce Philippe and come away with me?' he asked hungrily.

Alex was horrified, aware that she had provoked that question by speaking her mind. 'Gaston,' she said weakly. 'Gaston, I'm expecting Philippe's child.'

He went white to the black hairline, his eyes out of all control, his mouth shaking. 'Oh, God,' he groaned. 'Oh, God!'

Then he turned and galloped away without another word, crashing through the woodlands like a demented animal, while Alex sat on her horse and listened with pity and fear.

Slowly she rode back to Sarconne. The meeting with Gaston had been such a traumatic shock to her that as she tried to dismount she fainted, and came to her senses in the silken splendour of her own bedroom, with Lélie anxiously bent over her.

Alex's lashes fluttered weakly. 'Lélie ...' she whispered, her mouth trembling.

'Are you all right? You fainted ...'

Alex closed her eyes, sickened as the memory of Gaston came flooding back to her. Lélie rubbed her hands, exclaiming over their coldness, her gentle face filled with compassion.

Gisèle came into the room and gave her mother a tray. Lélie helped Alex to sit up, an arm around her shoulders, and held a cup of hot, sweet tea to her lips. Alex gratefully drank some, then gave a low moan as nausea filled her. She stumbled off the bed and ran to the bathroom. When she came back, white and shivering, Lélie was alone in the bedroom. She helped Alex back on to the bed, a little smile on her lips. She looked down into Alex's pale face with a delighted expression.

'You are going to have a baby!' She had leapt to that conclusion at once, Alex saw, and saw, too, that she had to admit it now. Lélie had had two babies; she would not be deceived.

'Don't tell Philippe,' Alex said huskily.

Lélie looked at her sharply. 'He will be over the moon!'

'Will he?' Alex looked at her, a little colour coming into her face. 'Oh, I feel so silly!'

'Silly?' Lélie was amused and puzzled. 'It is such wonderful news ... why silly?'

Alex was pink now, her eyes glazed. 'I ... I'm shy about it.'

'Well, he will soon begin to notice,' Lélie pointed out, openly teasing her now.

Alex ran a curious hand down her slender body. 'How soon will it show, Lélie?'

'When do you think it's due?' Lélie asked, frowning.

Alex thought. 'Next June,' she said, a little doubtfully.

'Then I doubt if it will show for some months,' Lélie said, her eyes smiling. 'Around Christmas time you will begin to be obvious.'

She brushed Alex's hair, sitting on the bed beside her. The door opened and Philippe came quickly into the room, his grey eyes anxious as he glanced towards the bed.

Alex felt her cheeks burn under his eyes. Lélie discreetly got up and vanished, closing the door quietly behind her.

'What happened?' Philippe asked her, coming to the bed and staring at her flushed, self-conscious face. 'Lélie rang to tell me you had fainted. You look perfectly well. You didn't hit your head or have a fall, did you?'

'No,' she whispered, biting her lip, trying to summon the courage to tell him her news but absurdly shy about it.

He pushed his hands into his pockets. 'You had been out riding,' he said flatly. 'Where did you go?'

'To the woods,' she said blankly, wondering why he was staring at her so fixedly.

'You met Gaston,' he said curtly.

Her colour deepened and tears filled her green eyes. She turned on to her face and broke into sudden wild tears, her body shaking. She was filled with the memory of Gaston's shock and pain as she told him she was having Philippe's child. Her emotional response to his pain was partly fuelled by her condition—her emotions seemed to have risen closer to the surface these days. She felt continually nervous and highly strung. She could laugh or cry easily without any real cause.

She was surprised to hear the door slam behind Philippe. Turning, her face wet with the easy yet painful tears, she stared at the empty room incredulously. Only then did she realise that, far from having told Philippe about her pregnancy, she had given him cause to believe she was in love with Gaston. She swayed as she stumbled off the bed, running to find him, to explain, to tell him about the baby, but as she reached the corridor she heard the door of the great hall slam and a moment later the sound of his car as it started.

She spent an anxious day, waiting for him to come home, mentally rehearsing the moment when she would tell him about the baby. During the later part of the afternoon she dressed carefully in one of her prettiest dresses. It would, she thought wryly, soon be impossible for her to wear any of them, so she might as well enjoy them while she could.

Philippe came home in a dark-browed mood, stalking into the Salon and helping himself to a drink without a word to her.

Alex nervously licked her lips, eyeing his dark profile. 'Er ... Philippe ...' she whispered, trying to find the words to tell him about the baby.

He turned, his glass in his hand. The grey eyes savagely surveyed her. 'I'm going to Paris tomorrow,' he said coldly. 'I'll be away for a few weeks.'

Her colour all died away. Elise was in Paris, she thought. The green eyes stared at him emptily. 'I see,' she said huskily.

'Do you?' Philippe's mouth twisted. 'Well, just in case you're hoping this leaves you free to meet Gaston as often as you like, I'm taking him with me.'

Her eyes widened. 'To Paris?' Then Philippe could not be meeting Elise, she thought wildly.

'To London,' Philippe said curtly. 'I'm sending him to London on business. This afternoon he told me he wanted to get away from the factory.' He stared at her in cold hostility. 'Gaston's conscience is presumably troubling him. He looked terrible this afternoon, worse than you did. You're breaking him up, Alex. He's in hell, poor devil.'

Her mouth shook helplessly. 'I know,' she whispered. 'Don't you think I don't know? I wish I'd never come here!'

'Then that makes two of us,' said Philippe, putting down his glass with a crash that made her jump. He turned and strode out of the room, leaving her trembling and sick.

He went early next morning without saying goodbye to her. She had lain awake half the night, feeling the tension and hostility between them like a sword. He had not spoken to her except in front of the servants, and then the words were aimed at a level just above her head, as if he could not even bear to look at her.

She was sick again when he had gone. Lélie fussed over her, ordering her to stay in bed, but as the day wore on Alex decided she would get up. She was bored in bed. Lélie clucked over that decision, but agreed, on condition that Alex rang the family doctor and got him to examine her.

He arrived in the late afternoon and spent a quarter of an hour talking to her, and smiling cheerfully as he confirmed the pregnancy.

'We can't be one hundred per cent certain until the test,' he told her. 'But unofficially, I think it is obviously a pregnancy.' He advised her on ways of combating the morning sickness, gave her a prescription for iron pills and a lecture on diet, then left, giving Lélie a little wink.

'This is going to cause some excitement,' he told her. 'Philippe will be thrilled.' Alex had admitted to him that she had not told her husband yet.

When he had gone, Lélie eyed her anxiously. 'You have not told Philippe? I thought last night ...'

Alex lied. 'I didn't want to raise his hopes if it was all a mistake,' she mumbled. 'I'll tell him after the tests are shown to be positive.'

Lélie smiled. 'Tests! I am certain already ... when a woman is sick every morning, there is only one reason.'

Alex laughed. 'I hope this sickness doesn't go on for too long—I've totally lost my appetite.'

'It will pass soon,' Lélie assured her.

That evening Marie St Georges rang her, excited and chattering. She had met the doctor who, in the strictest of confidences, had given her the news.

'I'm so thrilled,' Marie said, sounding it. 'Philippe will be so happy!'

'He's in Paris,' Alex told her. 'I'll tell him when he comes back.'

'I gather you're having bad morning sickness,' Marie went on. 'When I had that I used to eat a dry biscuit before I got up. It settles the stomach.'

'It makes me sick even to think of eating dry biscuits,' Alex groaned. 'I can't eat a thing at the moment.'

Marie laughed. 'Poor Alex! Never mind, it stops soon.'

'I hope so, or I may fade away to a shadow,' Alex said grimly.

Two days later she received confirmation of her pregnancy from the doctor, who sounded almost as pleased as if it were his child. 'Now, take care of yourself,' he advised. 'Rest for an hour every day and for the moment no more riding. After four months you can ride again for a little while if you like.'

To Lélie, Alex said ruefully, 'No more riding! I shall miss my rides.' It seemed a long time since she had begun to learn to ride with Gaston. She found it almost impossible to believe that there had been a time when she could not even ride a horse. Now she loved riding through the green fields and woods.

Lélie looked seriously at her. 'The doctor is right. During the first months it could be dangerous for you to ride, or to do anything strenuous.'

'It isn't an illness,' Alex complained. 'It's a natural event.'

'All the same,' said Lélie, 'please don't take any risks, Alex.'

All the servants appeared to know about the baby next day. There were smiles and knowing looks all round her as she went through her daily routine, and the happiness the event was giving percolated to her, boosting her morale. Knowing that Philippe was away, Marie insisted on driving over to Sarconne for the evening, and they talked and laughed together over the knitting patterns Marie had brought with her.

'Such tiny objects,' Alex groaned. 'My fingers are too clumsy. I shall never be able to knit anything so small.'

Marie had brought some delicate white wool with her too, and insisted on casting on the stitches required to make a pair of the minute baby booties. She watched critically as Alex clumsily tried to knit and laughed.

'Well, you must practise,' she said, shaking her head. 'You'll get the hang of it.'

They listened to a new record which Marie had brought with her, then talked lazily about the farm and Marie's family. Marie made Alex laugh as she retailed some funny anecdotes about life on the farm. It was impossible not to be envious of the warm family happiness which Marie shared with her husband and children. Alex ached with loneliness as she listened, wondering miserably if she would ever know such enveloping security. Could her marriage to Philippe ever become a real one? Would the coming child make some difference to what they shared?

Marie appeared to sense some of her depression. She looked at her affectionately, her head on one side. 'What is wrong, Alex? You are happy about the baby, aren't you?'

'Oh, yes,' Alex agreed at once, 'I'm very happy.'

'And Philippe will be so thrilled,' Marie prompted. 'He has waited so long to have a son.'

Alex's face saddened before she had time to cover her expression, and Marie shot her a worried look. 'My dear, if it is Elise who is bothering you ...' she said quickly, breaking off with a grimace.

Alex gave her a wide-eyed stare. So Marie had guessed! And who else knew? Did everyone in the district know what had been going on between Philippe and Elise? Humiliation and pain swept over her.

Marie put a hand over hers, squeezing her fingers. 'Don't look so upset. Elise is a greedy little cat. She made herself very obvious, throwing herself at Philippe like that. She didn't care who knew. Why Gaston didn't break her neck I'll never know. She had so many affairs quite openly, and he ignored them. But his own brother! It was shameful.'

'I'd rather not talk about it,' Alex said huskily.

'I understand how you feel,' Marie said in a quick, firm voice. 'But I'm convinced Elise merely annoyed and embarrassed Philippe. I never saw an ounce of encouragement from him, and then he married you, and got her out of the chateau and out of his hair ... so, you see, you don't need to take any notice of her. I know what a bitch she can be, and I've no doubt she tried to upset you, but you mustn't let her lies hurt you.'

'I won't,' Alex said very carefully. Marie meant well, and she was grateful to her for her kindness, but she did not know the truth. She yawned, and Marie gave a little exclamation.

'There, you are tired and I'm keeping you up. You must have as much rest as possible now, you know.'

Alex kissed her goodnight and watched her drive away, then with a feeling of weary misery she went in search of comfort in the only place she knew where she could be quite quiet and untroubled.

She stood on the donjon catwalk, leaning on the parapet, the warm darkness surrounding her, staring out towards the invisible whispering woodlands which were so rapidly becoming skeletal as the wind stripped away their leaves.

She remembered the day when she met Philippe and wondered how she could have failed to know why her body had received such a shock on seeing him. Every instinct in her had warned her about him, but she had been blind. Now she knew she loved him in a way which had never seemed possible—a love which governed her whole life, her mind and body, her heart and brain.

Gaston had confused the issue for a time. His affection had made her turn towards him because she already feared the hold Philippe was gaining on her. Once Gaston had left, she had had no defences against Philippe's dominance. After a brief, futile struggle, she had surrendered. She had not told him; she would never tell him. But he had everything of her now. No other man had ever come within a million light years of possessing her body and soul. Her love for Hal had been a rehearsal for this wild, destructive emotion. She had walked into the wind and waves long ago, a free spirit. Now she stood in the turmoil of the wind on the donjon and knew she was chained, captive, Philippe's possession. She closed her eyes in misery. He must never know. It would scald what was left of her pride if he ever guessed.

Driven by emotions which tore at her, she turned hurriedly and began to run down the donjon steps, forgetting the dangers of the twisting stairs, the steepness and darkness.

She caught at the rope handrail as her foot slipped, but it was not sufficient to halt her. With a hoarse cry she fell, her head striking the stone walls, her body wincing at the pain of the impact as she fell from stair to stair like a doll thrown down by an uncaring child.

CHAPTER EIGHT

SHE opened her eyes to a grey swirl of mist which slowly dispersed to show her a small white room and an unfamiliar face bending over her. The green eyes vaguely gazed into the strange face, without curiosity or even comprehension. Then the lids slowly fluttered down. Alex was too tired to think. She let the slow waters of oblivion close over her head without protest.

When she opened her eyes again the little white room was filled with wintry sunlight. She heard a voice beside the bed, a faint familiarity in it, and her eyes incuriously drifted to survey a pale, hard face from which grey eyes stared at her.

'Alex.' The voice was strangely husky. 'How are you?'

She knew that she was Alex. But she did not know this man and she did not want to speak to him. She looked away slowly, her lids closing, grateful for the waiting silence into which she fell.

She wanted to stay within that silence. It was a condition without pain, and she knew that when she emerged from it, pain waited for her.

It caught her as she awoke next time and she gave a low moan of protest and fear. A nurse was at her side at once, wiping her damp face, whispering to her. She felt the injection with a little groan, then the silence came back and she relapsed with a sigh into it.

She had lost all sense of place or time, of her own identity or her past. She was a creature being hunted by agony, and only in the peace of drugged sleep could she find escape. Sometimes when she was forced into wakefulness it was night. The lights hurt her eyes and she moaned incoherently for peace again, and it always came. A doctor grew familiar to her. He was a man with tired eyes and a quiet voice. She watched for him in the rare intervals of quiet between sleeps.

'How are you today, Alex?' he asked her, standing close, his face bent to avoid the necessity of her turning her head.

She had not spoken for days. Speech was too tiring, without necessity. She had nothing to say to anyone.

'Aren't you going to say hallo to me?' the doctor asked gently, smiling patiently at her.

Her white lips spaced the word slowly.

He smiled. 'That's better.' He looked up at something, and her weary eyes followed his, seeing for the first time the plastic tubing which fed her intravenously. He adjusted something, his eyes on it, then turned and smiled at her.

'You're looking better,' he said. 'Do you feel better?'

She was not sure about that. She felt resentment that anyone should ask her to make the effort of thinking about anything. Her brows knit irritably, fretfully.

The nurse appeared beside the doctor. Alex looked at her. They changed faces, these nurses. Sometimes it was one, sometimes another. The doctor was always the same.

'Would you like to see your husband?' the doctor asked her softly, watching her.

Alex stared, her brows confused. 'Husband?' Her lips silently shaped the word. She stared back at him. 'Who?' This time the word emerged in sound which startled her.

The tired face was careful as the doctor looked back

at her. 'You remember your husband, Alex?'

Her face reflected total bewilderment. The nurse withdrew and a man swam into her view. Alex looked at him blankly. He was a total stranger to her, a tall, commanding figure with a grey face and steel-grey eyes and black hair.

'Alex,' he said quietly, his hand touching her fingers.

She looked away from him to the watchful doctor, turning to him for protection from this stranger who seemed to know her. She felt a painful desire to sleep again. Something was worrying her. She was not sure what it was, but she did not want to think about it.

The green eyes pleaded with the doctor, knowing he held the key to that merciful oblivion. He stared at her thoughtfully. The strange man disappeared and the nurse came back. Alex felt the injection with that sigh of relief and gratitude, closing her eyes.

Slowly they weaned her from pain and sleep, the days passing in a mist of dull indifference. She began to speak, very carefully, drily, using her words sparingly because each one meant having to think, and that hurt. She grew to know each face intimately. Some she liked; others she did not.

One she did not like was the man with grey eyes who came rarely and looked at her without speaking.

The sight of him at her bedside made her head ache. She would close her eyes and lie still, hoping he would be gone when she opened them. Usually he was, and then she would sigh with relief.

She was swathed in bandages, she realised. She had shown no curiosity about what had happened to her, and nobody had offered to tell her anything.

Opening her eyes one day she found the room gay with foil chains and glittering stars. A frown creased her forehead. There were no nurses at her bedside today, which puzzled her. There was always someone there.

She stared at the decorated room, her green eyes wide. Then there was a movement and she let her eyes drift round, expecting to see a nurse, only to find the man she disliked there, a large bright package in his arms.

He put it on the side of the bed, drawing up a chair and sitting down right next to her.

Alex looked at the package.

'Shall I open it for you?' he asked quietly.

She lifted her green eyes to his face. 'Is it for me?'

It was the first time she had spoken to him, and the tension around his mouth relaxed.

'Yes,' he said, a smile coming into his hard features. '*Joyeux Noel*, Alex.'

'Christmas?' Of course, she thought, her eyes drifting back to the decorations. Silly to forget it. The quiet, empty world in which she had lain for so long had had no room for memories like Christmas.

She watched as the long fingers unwrapped the box and lifted the lid. She saw pale green drifts of lace and silk inside it. The man drew out a delicate, exquisite nightdress and held it up for her to see. A matching bedjacket was brought out next. Alex knew that she was wearing thick hospital issue winceyette. She looked delightedly at the lovely things, her mouth softening in a smile.

The man put them back in their box, then bent and touched his mouth briefly to hers.

The grey eyes looked into her green ones. 'Do you remember me now, Alex?'

She frowned. 'No,' she said, but she knew she was

lying. She did not want to remember him, but she knew that the memory lay just within reach if she cared to put out a hand for it. Instinct told her to leave those memories alone. They would hurt more than she could bear just now.

There was a brief silence. 'Do you remember Hal?' he asked huskily.

Alex's brows drew together. 'Who?' The name had a painful ring and that, too, was something she did not want to think about.

There was a longer silence. 'Gaston?' asked the man very gently.

Her lips trembled. 'No,' she said with a violence that denied her rejection. Her voice shook. 'Go away!' she moaned. 'Go away!'

Her eyes closed. When she opened them he had gone and the nurse was at her side, watching her quietly. She sighed with relief.

Slowly she began to gain ground. She forced herself, at their pleading, to eat a little. She was propped up to watch television. She listened to the radio. The man with grey eyes did not come for days and she was annoyed to find herself thinking about him, wondering why he had not come.

The doctor and nurses were as tactfully discreet as ever. They asked no questions, they told her nothing. The days went past slowly. Snow fell outside and the room darkened with a strange light. She was able to watch the crystal patterns reflected on the white walls when the sun came out and went in behind clouds. Her body was slowly healing. Some of the bandages came off and she began to look and feel normal again, a woman instead of a mummy.

One bright morning with snow still on the ground

she was carefully washed and had the delicate green nightdress put on, followed by the matching bedjacket. Was he coming today? she wondered, lying still in the bed, her shoulders propped by a pile of pillows. The nurse had brushed her red hair until it shone like a flame around her white face, had delicately dusted her skin with powder, put a light touch of green eyeshadow on her lids and a careful outline of lipstick on her pale lips.

She felt quite normal except that her mind still refused to come to life.

The door opened and she looked across the room, expecting to see the hard face and grey eyes.

Instead she saw a face which sent a shudder of pain through her. Her lips parted on a wild cry. 'Gaston!'

Before he had reached her, the tears were running down her face, the sobs tearing her slender body. Memory coursed through her like fire, burning and destroying. She was shaking, consumed with it.

Gaston sank on his knees beside the bed, his arms around her, his face disturbed.

'I'm sorry, *chérie*. I'm so sorry ...'

Her weeping would not stop, or the trembling of her body under the sheets. 'The waste of it,' she moaned wildly, unable to frame her words coherently. She thought of Gaston's marriage, his misery with Elise, his unrequited love for her. She thought of her need for Philippe. She thought of the thing she had been unable to face for days, and her cries were muffled with agony.

Gaston had no idea what to do. He knelt there, as white as she was, muttering huskily under his breath, patting her as if she were a sick child.

Someone lifted him away almost violently, bent over her and pulled her into his strong arms, the hard power of the body against her giving her a sort of peace. She leaned, sobbing, against the wide shoulder. 'I was going to have a baby,' she almost flung at him.

'I know,' he said harshly, his hands stroking over her body in a firm, gentle movement. 'Hush now, Alex. You're doing yourself no good.'

She pulled away to stare at him as if she hated him. He was so strong and alive. Her green eyes were wild. 'The baby,' she said bitterly. 'My baby.'

She knew she had reached the core of the pain. She felt it throb through her like the agony of death as her lips said the words. She had known all the time that the baby was gone. She had known even as she pretended to know nothing. She had not been able to admit the pain to her brain until now. She had reached that bitter core and must bear it.

Philippe held her tightly, stroking hair and back, his hands gentle. He said nothing, but he held her, and she leaned all her weight upon his strength, letting the grief tear at her at last.

When they gave her the injection she faded without a word into sleep, knowing she needed it now.

For several days she was kept under heavy sedation. She lay in a light doze during the daylight hours, slept heavily at night. When she emerged at last into reality she found her mind had coped somehow with the agony of her memories. She was dull and depressed but she was no longer in flight from reality.

Gaston visited her again the next day. She looked at him sadly, her green eyes shifting under the hungry black stare.

'How is Elise?' she asked politely.

His brows drew together. 'I am divorcing her,' he said flatly. 'She is living with a businessman in Lyons.

I should have done it years ago. Now she leaves me no choice.'

Alex absorbed that information slowly. 'What will you do?' she asked him.

'Philippe wants me to set up a London office,' he said. 'We sell our porcelain over in England through English firms, but now that England is in the Common Market it seems sense to open our own showroom in London.'

'It sounds very exciting, Gaston,' she said. Her green eyes grew shadowed. 'I hope you'll be happy in London. It's a lovely city.'

'Do you miss England?' he asked, watching her hungrily.

'Yes,' she admitted. 'It seems a long time since I was there. At first when I gained consciousness I couldn't understand why I kept hearing French around me.' Her mouth smiled, but her eyes had no light in them.

Gaston put a hand over hers. '*Chérie*, I must leave for London tomorrow. I shall not be able to visit you again. I think I know your answer, but I must ask you all the same ... will you come with me to England? Philippe will divorce you if you ask him, and we can be married over there and stay there for ever.'

She shivered, looking at him unhappily. 'I'm sorry, Gaston ...'

His face was haggard. 'No?' He tried to smile, his mouth twisting. 'Well, it is only what I expected, but ...' He broke off huskily. 'Remember, if you need me, I will always come, Alex.'

'Thank you, Gaston,' she said miserably, wishing he would go because she could not bear to see that look in his handsome, haggard face. She had brought him nothing but unhappiness and she bitterly regretted having met him.

When he had gone she drifted into unhappy thoughts, her head back on her pillow. The day moved on slowly in the usual routine with which she was now so familiar. In the evening, Philippe came to see her, carrying a large bouquet of daffodils.

She looked at them in disbelief. 'So early?'

'From the Channel Islands,' he told her, laying them on her locker.

He sat down beside her bed and the grey eyes scanned her pale face keenly.

'Gaston came to see you,' he said, as if prompting her.

Her green eyes fell away. 'Yes. He told me he's going to start a new office in London.'

'He leaves tomorrow,' Philippe said quietly.

'Yes, he said so.'

'Is that all he said, Alex?' Philippe asked.

She turned her head on the pillow. 'He said he was divorcing Elise because she's living with a man in Lyons,' she told him calmly.

'Yes,' Philippe said, his mouth wry. 'And what else, Alex?'

She met his gaze. 'Nothing.'

His brows drew together. 'I think there was,' he said flatly. 'He asked you to go to London with him and you refused. Why did you refuse, Alex?'

Her eyes widened. 'Have you forgotten I'm your wife? Do you want me to go, Philippe?'

He searched her green eyes. 'Did you want to go? That is all I want to know.'

'I don't want to do anything,' she said limply, her face quite cool.

He watched her, reading her dry indifference, the distance she had placed between herself and everything else in the world. 'Will you come back to Sarconne when they let you out of here?' he asked her quietly.

She had nowhere else to go. She had no home, no family, no friends in the world. Her face reflected her grim thoughts, and he stared at her eyes, reading them without difficulty.

His mouth compressed. 'I thought you had more spirit, Alex,' he said roughly.

She shrugged, her slender shoulders dispirited. 'I'm sorry if I'm boring you.'

He swore under his breath. 'Why do you always read the worst into what I say?' he asked bitterly.

Alex closed her eyes as if to shut him out. He was still for a few moments, although she could feel the grey eyes probing her white, shuttered face, as if he tried to read what lay behind it.

After a moment he moved away towards the window. She heard him tap on the glass with his fingertips, as if he were thinking hard. Then he said softly, 'Many of your friends have asked if they may soon come and visit you.'

She opened her eyes involuntarily in surprise. Friends? She turned her head to find him watching her intently.

'Would you like to see some new faces?' he asked carefully.

Her expression answered for her. 'Yes,' she said huskily, after a pause. 'Yes, I think I would.'

The first to come was Lélie, and when she walked in through the door Alex gave a little cry of pleasure, seeing the smiling, loving face framed in the open doorway. She held out her hands in a little gesture of

welcome, and Lélie came to the bed, her eyes filled
with tears, and bent to hug her, her arms going round
her.

'Oh, Lélie,' Alex whispered, her voice muffled against
the other woman's shoulder.

For a moment they stayed close, both half smiling,
half in tears. Then Lélie sat down on a chair and produced some fruit and some novels. 'English novels,' she
said, pleased with herself for the imaginative thought.

'How lovely,' said Alex, flipping over the pages. 'It's
so long since I read any English books. I've been reading French ones ...' She broke off, because that was a
lie. She had not been reading any books. Her mind
could not concentrate at all. She had been flicking over
French magazines, idly glancing at page after page,
taking in nothing of what she saw.

'Such beautiful flowers,' Lélie said, glancing around
the room. Philippe showered Alex with them, day after
day, as if he tried to bring the spring into her quiet
little cell, to disperse the grey routine of the hospital
with fragrance and colour.

'Yes,' she said indifferently. She did not want to think
of Philippe. 'How is Gisèle?' she asked, her tone changing.

'She is very well,' Lélie told her. 'She sent her love.
She misses you. She is helping me with the work, but
she is longing to have you back home and be able to
look after you again.'

Alex asked after the other servants one by one,
naming their names in a sort of roll call, forgetting
none of them, and Lélie smilingly replied. 'They will
all be so pleased that you asked after them,' she said.
'We've all missed you. The house has been empty without you, Alex.'

Alex smiled at her, believing the quiet tone. It was like being part of a family, she thought. Without noticing or realising it, over the months since she arrived in France she had become part of them all, and they had become part of her. She belonged with them. It was a wonderful feeling.

'When do you think they will let you come home?' Lélie asked eagerly.

'I don't know,' said Alex, trying to sound light. 'They never tell me anything. Very secretive, these doctors. They smile and chat to me, but they keep their own counsel.'

The nurse appeared, smiling primly, and Lélie was firmly but gently banished. She stood up reluctantly, bent to kiss Alex on the cheek. 'I'll come again when they let me,' she said, and Alex smiled back at her lovingly.

'Oh, yes, please do,' she said, meaning every word of it.

When Philippe came in that evening he brought a present with him, his grey eyes smiling as she unwrapped it. 'Cassettes,' she said, her face taken aback.

He produced a cassette player. 'Now you can have music whenever you like,' he said. 'I don't know why I didn't think of it before. I've brought you some English folk songs.'

It was a Kathleen Ferrier recording, the pure clear voice very moving as she sang the old songs unaccompanied, and Alex felt tears rise behind her lids, but her mouth closed, refusing to release them, to let the emotion flow freely.

She was conscious of Philippe's watchful gaze, and guessed he had brought the recording deliberately. A test? she wondered. Was he trying to find out how homesick she was?

She was very homesick, she admitted, lying there on her pillows. A split mind was a painful business. Part of her longed for England, for the sea, the quiet fields, the bustle of London. Part of her ached to see the conical towers of Sarconne, the dark woods, the wide white road which led to the main door.

Philippe got up to go and came to the bed to kiss her. She turned her cheek as usual, her face cool, but he lifted her chin with his finger and took her mouth hard, his lips abruptly hungry, as if he was angrily unable to restrain himself.

She shivered, feeling the hunger reach out towards her, and he at once moved away and went without a word.

Marie came two days later. She stood in the door, smiling, and Alex felt her spirits lift. They laughed, their eyes meeting, and five minutes later Alex was lying back listening, enraptured, as Marie chattered of the weather, the farm, the new calves, the silage, all the details of her daily life. Affection graced the mundane gossip. Alex was hungry for it as if she had been locked away for years and could not hear enough. Only once did the warm happiness falter. Marie, laughing, mentioned her youngest child, and something deep inside Alex winced. She gave no outward sign, she thought, but Marie was sensitive, aware of her lapse, and she stopped talking suddenly, a look of dismay on her face. Alex gave her a weary little smile.

'It doesn't matter.' The words were vague, but she wanted to convey her acceptance to Marie.

'Oh, Alex, I'm so sorry,' Marie said huskily.

'Never mind.' Alex could have laughed at the weak idiocy of the phrases one used to convey such delicate thoughts.

Marie held her hand tightly. For a moment they were silent, then Alex said, 'Tell me about the village ... are they still arguing about the hall?'

Marie gratefully plunged into a giggling tale about the local row which had been going on for months, and Alex laughed as she listened, eager to hear every little detail.

After that, the days passed very fast. She had visitors enough now. Hardly a day passed without someone coming in to see her, and she was happy to see them all.

'I gather your room is becoming an extension of Sarconne,' Philippe said wryly. 'Everyone I meet has been in to see you. You aren't getting bored with them all, I hope?'

'I love to see them,' she said honestly. 'What else do I have to think about, lying here all day?' She moved restlessly. 'When can I leave here, Philippe? They tell me nothing. I can get up now. They let me walk about and sit up for a few hours every day. Surely I don't need to stay here much longer?'

'That's up to you,' he said. 'Do you want to come home?'

Alex did not hesitate. 'Yes,' she said. She had wanted to for a long time, waiting for them to tell her she could go, bored with the four walls around her.

A week later he collected her and they drove through the spring countryside while she stared and stared, her eyes drinking in the bright new leaves, the mystery of the earth renewing itself, the colour creeping from field to field as the cool, bright sun shifted across the sky. The road wound from hill to valley, revealing new vistas of wood and pasture, and Alex felt like Lazarus reborn. It was all so startlingly beautiful she could have cried. She felt tensed, like a coiled spring. Her hands clenched in her lap.

When the conical towers flashed through trees towards her she could not restrain a brief intake of breath.

Philippe glanced at her watchfully.

She felt his eyes on her and turned her head slowly. The grey eyes searched her pale face.

'All right?' he asked huskily.

'Yes,' she said, wondering how to convey the feeling which was sweeping into her.

She felt one word beating in her brain. Sarconne. They had reached the road and it lay before them, magical as a vision, the grace and elegance of it unbelievable in the bright spring sunlight. Tears pricked at her eyes as she felt it reaching out to her to pull her towards it. She had felt that so often before with fear and dismay. She had thought it would consume, engulf, destroy her. How many times had she hated it, sensing it to threaten her individuality? That beauty had seemed a threat, a menace. Now she felt so differently. The beauty and warmth drew her like a moth towards light. She knew Sarconne now; she belonged to it. Within those walls lay all she knew of love and shelter. Lélie, Gisèle and all the others were waiting there for her. She was no longer the unwanted, despised intruder, the English nobody who had felt herself an outcast. She was part of the beauty, the ritual of love which was Sarconne. She was coming home.

They rattled over the drawbridge and she looked down at the dry moat. They drew up in the courtyard and she looked up at the glittering leaded windows, listened to the silvery playing of the fountain. Philippe came round to lift her from the car, but she said quietly, 'Let me walk, please.'

He stood back, his face expressionless.

She swayed slightly, still shaky on her feet. The door into the great hall stood open. They were all inside, leaving her and Philippe alone discreetly for the moment, but waiting.

Slowly she walked towards the door. Philippe moved at her side, not touching her, but watching in case she should falter.

Pleasure and laughter broke out as she went into the hall. They embraced her one after another, their eyes filled with affection, and then Philippe silently lifted her, like a child, his face grim.

'This is too tiring,' he said to them all, and they scattered, stricken with remorse, while he carried her up to the Royal Chamber.

Gisèle followed discreetly and Philippe left her alone with the girl. Alex was almost too tired to move. She let Gisèle undress her languidly, her eyes too bright in her pale face. Gisèle brushed her hair carefully, helped her into a bedjacket, slid her between the cool, lavender-scented sheets.

There was a bright flush on Gisèle's face as she asked if there was anything she could do.

'No, thank you,' said Alex, then with a small smile, 'Unless I could have a cup of tea?' She wanted one badly. In the hospital it had been coffee all the time. Their idea of tea had been a very pale straw-coloured brew which tasted of nothing in particular.

Gisèle beamed. 'Lélie said you would want one!'

Alex laughed at her. 'Lélie knows me.' There was fierce pleasure in saying that.

Gisèle hesitated, a flush on her cheeks. 'I'm so glad you're home,' she said quickly. 'I've missed doing things for you.' Then she had gone, embarrassed by her own words, and Alex lay back, smiling on her pillows.

Her eyes flickered slowly over the room. The silken splendour was now so familiar, so real.

Philippe brought her the tea himself and sat watching her drink it. Lélie had sent up some English biscuits. The thought touched her, and she forced herself to eat two, although she was not hungry. Philippe watched her nibbling at them with a wry expression.

'Lélie went into town to get those specially,' he told her.

'I guessed that,' she said.

'I know you did,' Philippe murmured.

Something odd about his voice puzzled her. She looked at him enquiringly. He was frowning.

'Don't be too kind, Alex,' he said abruptly. 'Think of yourself for once. In the long run it is cruel to be kind.'

She was taken aback. She did not understand. Her green eyes told him so and his mouth tightened. 'Never mind,' he said, getting up and removing her cup. 'Go to sleep. You look worn out.'

She snuggled down between the cool scented sheets, content and exhausted. 'It's so nice to be home,' she said, her eyes closing. 'So nice to be back at Sarconne.'

There was a long silence. She did not have the energy to lift her lids again to see what Philippe was doing. After a moment or two she heard the door close quietly and she let sleep engulf her.

CHAPTER NINE

BEING back at Sarconne seemed to give Alex a new lease of life. As if the old walls stored a source of untapped energy she felt it flowing into her, renewing her mind and body. She spent the first few days in bed, at Philippe's insistence. The doctor came to visit her often, smiling complacently at her obvious health.

He had seen her in hospital, and now she looked a different girl. 'You're really on the mend,' he assured her, but she had not needed to be told that. She had felt it herself.

Gradually she was allowed up for longer and longer periods. The spring blossomed beyond the old walls, breaking into bud and blossom on the trees, sending a great green wave crashing over the woodlands as the leaves unfurled and the birds nestled among them. Philippe took her for drives through the narrow roads, parking quietly for a while so that she could stroll along the woodland paths and see the renewal of the spring at close hand.

The injuries she had suffered had faded. Her broken bones had knit healthily, her young skin had regained its bloom. Fresh air and exercise put back colour into her face and her eyes were alive once more, her smile frequent. She slipped back into the household routine as if she had never been away. Marie visited her and gossiped. They drove to the little market town together, arguing over vegetables and fish on the busy stalls, drinking coffee at the little café on the corner of the market square.

There was one question in Alex's mind, but she did not know how or who to ask—would she ever be able to bear a child again? The thought persisted, nagging at the back of her mind. Philippe no longer shared her room. They lived under the same roof, polite and friendly strangers. He occasionally kissed her lightly as if he were her brother; but he never showed any sign of needing more than that, and she wondered if the attraction between them was quite dead.

Marie gave a dinner party for her just after Easter. Philippe and Alex drove there silently through the dusk. She wore the white dress they had chosen together in Paris. It was the first time she had been out for months and she felt odd.

Pierre teased her lightly over the dinner table. 'Eat some more of this cheese ... you need fattening up. Don't you agree, Philippe?'

The grey eyes slid over her briefly. 'She is rather thin,' he agreed quietly.

'Fashionably slender,' Marie insisted, giving her husband a reprimanding look.

After dinner Pierre sat beside her on the couch, showing her photographs of the holiday he and Marie had taken last year in the Alps. The snow-covered peaks seemed all the same to her, but she smiled over them, while Marie clicked her tongue and protested that Pierre was being boring.

'I'm not a bit bored,' she said, smiling at Pierre. The homely atmosphere was pleasantly relaxing. She was not bored at all and her green eyes smiled at him.

During the rest of the evening they listened to a new long-playing record, light romantic music which soothed without sinking below the surface of the mind. When they left Alex was sleepy without being painfully tired, and she kissed Marie warmly. 'And me,' Pierre claimed, slightly drunk. She turned her face smilingly and he kissed her. Marie giggled and made a face.

'He's drunk!'

Alex grinned at her. 'Just a little,' she said.

They understood each other. Marie did not mind Pierre's little flurry of flirtatiousness and Alex did not take it seriously.

Philippe put her into the car and drove away, his face expressionless. She hummed the romantic music under her breath, lying back in her seat, feeling warm and happy.

When Sarconne shot into view her eyes widened with pleasure. She sighed and Philippe glanced at her.

Her smile glimmered in the darkness of the car. 'Pierre isn't the only one who's drunk too much,' she said lightly. 'It was very good wine.'

When she got out of the car she was yawning. Lélie had waited up for them, excited by this first venture into normal living. She gave Alex's flushed, smiling face a pleased look.

'I can see you've enjoyed yourself. Good meal, was it?'

'Good wine,' said Alex, laughing.

'Oh, like that, is it?' Lélie laughed back. 'Bed for you, my lady!'

Alex looked at Philippe through her lashes. 'I'm too tired to walk upstairs,' she said, urging him silently to carry her.

Lélie looked at him expectantly, her eyes tender. He glanced from one to the other of them, his mouth wry, then calmly lifted Alex into his arms and moved away with her. She moved closer to him, a hand sliding round his neck, nestling against him sleepily.

He carried her into the bedroom and deposited her on the bed in a manner far removed from gentleness. She looked at him in surprise, her eyes questioning.

'I'm in no mood for games, Alex,' he said flatly, moving out of the room without looking at her.

She felt rejection burn in her cheeks. She had made an open move towards him, her courage fuelled by the wine she had drunk, and he had deliberately refused her. The green eyes glowed with pain and anger. He could not have made it clearer. He did not want her. He had married her to hurt and taunt Elise, and now Elise had gone, and Philippe had no further use for her. She remembered his asking her if she was sure she did not want to go to England with Gaston. Had he hoped she would solve the problem herself by leaving him?

She lay awake for a large part of the night, wrestling with the problem of the future. She had too much pride to stay at Sarconne if Philippe wanted her to go, but she was aware that her physical health was not yet sufficiently recovered for her to leave and get a normal job in London. She still suffered from headaches now and then, she was still easily tired, her body rapidly using up her stores of energy. She would not be able to make a life for herself until she was able to face the world alone on her own two feet.

Two weeks later Philippe looked at her across the dinner table and said quietly, 'I have to go to England, Alex. Gaston has set up the necessary arrangements for the new office, but I have to go over there myself and check them all. Would you like to come?'

She raised her green eyes, her face cool. 'Thank you, I would like that.'

She made no other comment; her mind had already made the decision for her. She would not be returning to Sarconne with him. She wondered if he was aware of it. Something in the brief look he gave her as he said goodnight later made her suspect he did.

It was hard over the next few days to go about her day's routine knowing that she would soon be saying goodbye to everything at Sarconne for ever. A poignant emotion troubled her every waking moment. She wanted to cry. The green eyes looked over-bright, the soft mouth trembled, whenever she felt unobserved.

She had come here hating it, fearing it. She would leave with bitter regret.

When they left, she had to control herself strongly to stop the tears from bursting out. As it was, she held Lélie tightly as she whispered goodbye, her slender body shaking as she felt the older woman kiss her cheeks. She felt as if she were saying goodbye to her own mother, and the unspoken truth which lay between them was bitter.

Lélie looked at her anxiously, reading her pale face without guessing the depths of sadness which lay behind it.

'Are you sure you are well enough for such a journey?' she asked. She turned to Philippe. 'She does not look strong enough, Philippe.'

He gave her a brief, unsmiling look. 'I'll take good care of her,' he said curtly, helping Alex into the car, as though he were afraid she might not come.

She waved goodbye to Lélie for as long as she could see her, then turned and sat silently, her hands tightly clenched in her lap. The tears were dammed now. She did not mean to cry again.

The journey was tiring. She was almost limp with exhaustion when they booked into their London hotel. She stood at Philippe's side by the reception desk, her head drooping on her thin neck, her bright hair blazing around her white face.

As they walked towards the lift she heard a voice which stopped her in her tracks.

She turned, incredulous, and her eyes searched across the carpet-lined foyer. Hal stood by an open door, talking to a short man in a dark suit.

Philippe had halted too. She slowly looked round at him, her green eyes accusing.

'You knew he worked here!'

She did not doubt it. Something in his expression warned her. He lifted his wide shoulders in a shrug. 'I thought you might like to see him again.'

Trying to get rid of her by any means in his power, Alex thought angrily. He must be desperate, grasping at such straws. Did he despise her so much that he thought she would run back into Hal's arms after what she knew about him?

She walked into the lift and stood without speaking beside him, her face averted, because if she met his eyes she might reveal just how angry she was with him. They had separate rooms. She left him and walked into her own and sat down on the chair by the window, her head throbbing. After washing, she got into a night-dress and fell into the bed, her eyes closing immediately. The knock on the door barely ruffled the surface of her mind. After a pause the door opened and Philippe walked across to the bed. Alex slowly raised her lids to look at him vaguely.

'Are you ill?' he asked quickly, moving to her side.

'Leave me alone,' she muttered. 'I want to sleep.' She was too tired to hide her anger with him. The green eyes threw hostility towards him before they closed again.

Alex slept through the evening and throughout the night, waking with a faint headache in the grey London dawn, hearing the surge of traffic with a sense of surprise. She was by now so accustomed to waking up in the silence of the French countryside that the sea-like roar of the roads below the hotel windows made her feel oddly alarmed.

Getting up, she took her time in bathing and dressed carefully. So far she had not a plan in her head. She had to make plans. She needed a job and somewhere to live, and with her background she knew perfectly well that that meant a hotel job. It was the only life she knew.

By the time she was ready it was still very early. She decided not to wait for Philippe, but to go down to breakfast alone. Crossing the foyer, she found herself face to face with Hal.

His face flushed a deep red as their eyes met. He paused, his eyes flicking over the expensive, well-cut dress she wore.

There was, though, no surprise in his face. She guessed that he had known that she and Philippe were in the hotel.

'How are you, Alex?' he asked levelly, his next words confirming her suspicions. 'I saw your name in the register. Is it the first visit you've made back to England since your marriage?'

'Yes,' she said quietly.

'I hope it worked out for you,' he said. 'It was a very sudden business, a bolt from the blue.'

She flushed. 'Yes,' she said again, evading the question. 'What about you, Hal?' Are you married now?'

He looked surprised. 'Me? No, of course not.' He looked as if she had insulted him, his eyes angry.

She was suddenly irritated with him. 'What? Surely one of the lovely ladies you flirted with so happily would have done?' Her tone was sarcastic and Hal looked taken aback.

'What on earth are you talking about?'

'The rest of the staff were very loyal to you until I broke our engagement,' she informed him quietly. 'Then they filled me in on some details I seemed to have missed.'

He was beginning to look unhappy, his eyes hangdog. 'It never meant a thing, Alex,' he said earnestly. 'I was only keeping guests happy, trying to make friends. None of them meant a thing, surely you believe that? It was you I wanted to marry.'

She saw that he was serious, that he did not think his behaviour had been so inexcusable. Hal saw life from his own point of view. He had probably never done more than flirt gently with any of them. Except, possibly, sad little Deirdre, who had been hungry for warmth and caring, and had demanded more of him than Hal had meant to give. She stared at him, almost sorry for him. He was a male butterfly, flitting from flower to flower without meaning to linger. No doubt he had thought that in choosing her as a life's partner he had paid her an enormous compliment which, by running off with another man, she had thrown back in his teeth.

'Take my advice, Hal,' she said wryly. 'Next time you meet a girl you want to marry, remember, they like sole rights in their men, not a small share.'

Half laughing, she turned away and went into the diningroom, leaving Hal staring after her with an affronted expression.

Philippe joined her just as she finished her light breakfast. He gave her a quick, unsmiling look. 'Did you sleep well?'

'Yes, thank you,' she said. 'What are you planning to do today?'

'I thought we would call on Gaston,' he said, pouring himself a cup of coffee.

'There's no need for me to come with you,' she said quietly. 'I'll do some shopping.'

The grey eyes surveyed her sharply. 'Gaston would be hurt if you avoided him altogether,' he said. 'You have to see him some time or another. He is my brother, after all.'

'I expect I shall see him some other time,' she said, her eyes blank. She planned to look for a job this morning, taking advantage of Philippe's absence.

'Are you afraid to see him?' Philippe asked curtly.

She met his eyes angrily. 'No! Why should I be?'

He shrugged. 'Then why not come?'

Her mouth set firmly. 'Very well,' she said, seeing that he would go on probing if she refused. She would have to put off finding a job until later.

In the taxi on the way to Gaston's flat, Philippe asked coolly, 'Have you met up with your ex-fiancé yet?'

'I ran into him on the way to breakfast,' she said indifferently.

He leaned back, his eyes on the pavements outside the window. 'And?'

'And what?' she challenged.

He turned his head and her eyes flashed angrily at him. 'What did you expect to happen? Was I supposed to fall into his arms and beg him to take me back? Sorry, it didn't happen. I couldn't care less if I never set eyes on him again.'

Philippe made no response, the grey eyes penetrating. Alex felt like hitting him. He sat there with that impenetrable expression, his mind hidden from her, giving nothing away. Did he think she was a fool? He had brought her to London to find her another man as if she were a lost kitten he was trying to give away. Well, he needn't bother. She could take care of herself. She had done until she met him, and she could manage perfectly well again.

Gaston opened the door of his flat with a tight smile. He had changed in the months since she last saw him. A London pallor seemed to have crept over his skin. He looked different—less French, perhaps. He was wearing casual English clothes which made a distinct alteration in his appearance. He greeted them quietly, his face as expressionless as Philippe's, his eyes barely touching her.

He offered them coffee, left them in the small sitting-room of the flat while he made it. Philippe prowled around, touching books and ornaments.

'Why don't you help Gaston with the coffee?' he asked, his back to her.

'For God's sake, Philippe!' she burst out furiously.

He stiffened. 'What's the matter?'

She stared at his back, seeing a tide of dark red creeping up the back of his neck.

'Any minute now you'll be giving me away with a set of porcelain,' she snapped. 'There's no need to find me a home, Philippe. I can manage perfectly well without your help. For the record, I don't want either Hal or your brother. I've already decided what I shall do, and it doesn't involve either of them.'

He turned slowly, his eyes fixed on her face, his expression unreadable.

'What does it involve?' he asked curtly.

'That's my business. Just stop trying to push me into another man's arms!'

'Is that what I've been doing?' he asked drily.

'Isn't it?' Her green eyes challenged him.

Gaston came in at that moment with the coffee on a tray and stopped, seeing their expressions. There was a strained silence.

After a pause he put down the tray on the small table in the centre of the room and politely asked Alex if she took sugar and cream.

'Cream, no sugar,' she said, watching him add the cream.

He passed her the cup and she sat down on a chair, her eyes on her cup, wondering how she was going to bear the situation much longer.

'You're looking better,' he said gently as he stood beside her chair, stirring his own coffee. 'Are you quite recovered now?'

'Yes,' she said, giving him a polite little smile. They were suddenly strangers to each other, the emotions of the past between them like a great dark abyss. 'How are you finding London?'

'Exciting,' he said. 'A little alarming at first, but I've begun to make friends.'

'Have you heard from Elise?' she asked, rushing in where fools always go. 'Is the divorce going through?'

'Yes,' he said. 'The divorce is settled. She wants to marry her businessman. He's rich and lavishes his money on her. Elise is having the time of her life. Her one worry is that I won't get the divorce pushed through before the fellow tires of her. She nags me by letter to get a move on.'

He sounded wry, indifferent, as if Elise no longer bothered him at all, so her question had not hurt or angered him. He seemed quite cheerful about divorcing Elise.

Alex glanced at Philippe to try to read his reactions to the news about his brother's wife, and found him staring at her, his grey eyes narrowed.

She finished her coffee and put down the cup. 'Thanks for the coffee, Gaston,' she said, giving him a smile. 'I'll leave you two to talk business now. I've got some shopping to do.'

'I was hoping you would have lunch here,' he said, looking surprised.

'Why not?' Philippe cut in quickly. 'You could do your shopping and come back, Alex.'

'I thought I would have lunch in the West End,' she said, her eyes not quite meeting his. 'Some other time, Gaston.' She moved to the door and he followed her, looking concerned.

Getting her alone in the small hall, he murmured anxiously, 'Things are well between you and Philippe, chérie? I did not cause a rift between you, I hope? I would hate to have harmed you even more than I did.'

'Please, Gaston,' she broke in, looking agitated. She could not bear to mention the past; it still hurt too much. 'Believe me, you're not responsible for anything.' She went out of the door quickly, longing to get away.

As she walked down the stairs Philippe came after her, his face oddly pale. 'Where are you going, Alex?' he demanded, his voice lowered.

'Shopping, I told you,' she retorted, her eyes avoiding the penetration of his grey gaze.

He looked at her uncertainly. 'How long will you be?'

She shrugged. 'A few hours. What are you going to be doing?'

'I have to talk to Gaston, have lunch with him, then we were going to view the site of the new office and showroom,' he said.

'What time will you be back at the hotel?' she asked calmly. If he was going to be out all afternoon she might be able to leave the hotel before he came back. If she got a job fixed up this morning, she could leave at once. She was beginning to find the strain of being in his constant company far too much to bear. She had to get away before the tension showed on her face.

He looked down at her then away, his face unreadable. 'Around six-thirty,' he said idly. 'Maybe later. I'll be back in time for dinner, I imagine.'

She nodded. 'I'll see you later, then.'

He stood still, watching her move away, and she felt her heart wincing as each step took her further and further away from him. She knew she could not face the prospect of saying a goodbye to him. She would have to vanish without a word. The realisation that she would probably never see him again was a bitter one, but she held her head high and gave no sign of it on her pale face as she turned into the busy London street.

She went to an agency which specialised in finding temporary jobs for hotel staff. She was lucky. She got a position right away. Taking a taxi, she saw the hotel manager, was given an eager welcome and given the job. Her explanation that she had been working in France was accepted. She gave the references from the past cheerfully, guessing that by the time they had had the English replies they would not bother about writing to France.

'I'm looking for a room at the moment,' she explained, and was offered a room in the hotel at cut rates, which she accepted. Then she had lunch and did some shopping before going back to the hotel.

She had not brought many clothes with her. She packed quickly and neatly, listening with some anxiety for any sound which might betray Philippe's return to his room. At last she was ready. She wrote him a brief note explaining that she was going, then took her case and walked out into the corridor. She bent and pushed the note under his door, then turned to go, her heart heavy.

A gasp of shock came from her as his door opened and he caught her arm in a fierce grip, jerking her back towards him. 'I thought so,' he said between his teeth. 'No, you don't, Alex. You're not walking out on me with a few polite words.'

She faced him, her face pale, her eyes nervous. 'It's the best way,' she said huskily. 'We should never have got married—we both know that.'

He removed her case from her hand and pushed her into his room, closing the door and leaning against it, staring at her.

'Where did you think you were going?' he asked.

'I've got a job in a hotel,' she told him. 'I'll be all right. It's a good job with a nice room and fair wages.'

His eyes were brilliantly angry as, almost white with rage, he moved towards her, and she backed, her heart in her mouth.

'Why don't you admit it?' she flung furiously. 'Our marriage was a stupid mistake. You've been trying to think of a way of ending it for months.'

'Have I?' he asked sardonically.

'I'm not blind,' she told him bitterly. 'First you find Hal, which must have taken some doing, then I get Gaston offered to me on a plate ... well, I don't want either of them!'

'Then that's both of them out of the running,' he said coolly, watching her. 'Which leaves me.'

Alex's colour deepened, a humiliated surge of emotion bringing a fierce brightness to her green eyes. She forced herself to glare back at him, holding herself very stiffly.

'You're not even in the race,' she said huskily.

Philippe's eyes flared with temper. 'Aren't I, by God?' He took three strides, seizing her by the slender shoulders, dragging her hard against him, the grey eyes leaping as they looked down into her face.

'Let me go,' she said hoarsely. 'I hate you to touch me!'

'That wasn't the impression you've been giving me since our marriage,' he said between his teeth.

Her eyes went fever-bright with shame and pain. 'You bastard,' she said shakily.

His eyes were dark, tormenting, as they moved over her. 'Am I to believe that any man could have had the passion you showed me in bed, Alex?' he asked sharply.

She flinched, her face turned away. 'I detest you,' she said through shaking lips.

'That's too bad,' he said harshly. 'Because I'm not letting you go, now or ever.'

'You don't want me,' she muttered.

'Shall I show you how much I want you?' he asked, the rage going out of his face and a smiling mockery coming into the grey eyes.

Surprise made her look at him, and before she could back away his mouth trapped her, his kiss sensually demanding, burning along her nerve ends, carrying her away on a full tide of passion. It was so long since he had made love to her, she lacked the ability to control her own response. Her struggles were over before they started. She swayed in his arms, her head dizzy, her mouth turned up towards him. The violent hunger with which he consumed it shook her to her depths. The strong, commanding hands curved over her bodice, caressing the high breasts gently, their slow touch arousing.

'Philippe,' she groaned under his lips. 'Don't do this to me.' Her trembling voice begged for pity. He did not love her, but she knew she would never find the strength to deny him if he wanted her.

'Stop me, then,' he whispered, his lips moving to wander down her throat, sending a shiver along her spine. 'Do you believe I want you now, or do you need more evidence?'

'Don't make fun of me,' she said bitterly.

He lifted his head. The grey eyes blazed down at her. 'Why the hell should I make fun of you? I find nothing remotely funny in the situation. You've been driving me out of my mind for weeks, Alex!'

She stared at his face, thrown into confusion. What was he saying? A frown twisted her pale forehead. What was in that cold, clever mind of his?

'I don't understand you,' she flung at him. 'I've never been able to understand you.'

'Then it's time you started to,' he said drily. 'Because I've no intention of losing you, Alex. You belong to me and we've got to learn to understand each other.'

He slid his arms under her, lifting her off the ground

and up against his chest, carrying her across the room
to the bed. When he lowered her on to it and lay down
beside her, she shivered, knowing that she did not have
the strength to resist him if he wanted her, even though
it would be agony to let him make love to her when he
did not love her.

He lay on his side, sliding a hand under her bright
hair, turning her head towards him, his fingers silkily
stroking her nape.

'I told you that you were blind about men, my
darling,' he said in a deep, husky voice. 'I fell in love
with you the first moment I set eyes on you.'

She stiffened, staring at him incredulously, her eyes
widening in disbelief.

Philippe's mouth twisted. 'You look stunned,' he
said drily. 'I felt much the same myself, watching you
... you ran along that groyne so lightly, like a ballet
dancer, with your lovely hair flying in the wind, and I
couldn't take my eyes off you ... I knew how I felt
from the first. When you fell into my arms it was like
getting a present from fate. I'm surprised you didn't
hear my heart beating like a drum.'

She had, she remembered, her mind thrown back to
their first meeting. She had heard a sound like thunder
and wondered if it was her heart or his.

'When fate threw me another chance later, and we
saw your fiancé with another woman, I took it un-
scrupulously. I'd made it my business to find out all I
could about you and the man you were going to marry.
I was as jealous as hell of him before I set eyes on him.'

Alex stared up at his dark, intent face, listening with
a sensation of total astonishment. She had never for a
moment suspected his feelings. Was he telling her the
truth?

'I saw my chance at once and I took it,' he said wryly. 'You were too shaken to consider my motives and I was able to get your engagement broken and persuade you to marry me at once. I couldn't risk going back to France and leaving you around where some other man could make off with you. I had to marry you out of hand.'

'I don't believe it,' she whispered, already hoping he would convince her.

'I'll make you believe me,' he said, running a finger down her flushed cheek, making her pulses leap by the light touch. 'I'm crazy about you.' His voice was deep and shaking. 'Even the few nights after our marriage before we got to Sarconne I had to fight not to make love to you. I wanted you in my bed so badly, Alex, but I was going to be patient. The night we arrived and I came up to find you wide awake, waiting for me, I couldn't help myself.'

There was a note in his voice which was too convincing to be assumed. She stared, searching his eyes. They were leaping with silvery fire, passion and pleading in them.

'Elise,' she said, suddenly, frowning.

'Good God,' he said scathingly. 'I loathed the little bitch!'

She gave a low, incredulous sound.

'Any fool could see what she was like,' he told her sharply. 'I saw right from the start what sort of life my unfortunate brother was going to have with her, and I was proved right. She had affairs with other men from the beginning. At one stage she chased me, but I made it clear what I thought of her, so she hated me ... she let Gaston think I'd had her to hurt him. I told him frankly what I thought of her, but Gaston was too sick to believe me by then. She was like a vampire, eating him whole. He was quite a different character before he married Elise. Charming, gay, full of life ... she warped his mind.'

'Why did you let me think you loved her, then?' she asked, staring at him.

'It stopped you from asking too many questions about my reason for marrying you,' he said, his mouth wry. 'I've got my pride, Alex. I wasn't prepared to reveal my heart to you when I knew you loved another man ... remember, when we met you were still in love with your fiancé.'

'Yet you deliberately threw me into Hal's company on this trip,' she said slowly.

'I felt guilty about all that you'd been through because of me,' he said, his voice filled with pain. 'The baby, the accident ... you seemed to hate me when you started to recover. I used to come to see you in that damned hospital and you would shut your eyes and ignore me.'

'I couldn't bear to think about you,' she admitted. 'It hurt too much. I couldn't face it for a long while.'

'Do you think I didn't know that?' He sounded as if he had shared her agony of mind. 'I hated myself.'

'Why didn't you give me a sign you felt like this long ago?' she asked him quietly to jolt him out of his pain.

Philippe groaned. 'Pride,' he muttered grimly. 'The pride of the devil, Lélie would say. I couldn't bear to expose myself to your mockery.'

'Is that what you thought I would do? Mock you?' She regarded him incredulously.

'You didn't love me then,' he said, his jaw tight. 'You still cared for that swine in England. I used to see you gazing at nothing with a dreamy look on your face, and I seethed with jealousy.'

Alex looked at him through her lashes. 'You covered it very well. You seemed to hate me at times.'

'When you're in love with someone who doesn't love you, hate can come pretty close to love,' he said harshly.

'Yes,' she said, remembering how she had felt she hated him at times.

'I thought you would learn to forget your fiancé,' Philippe muttered. 'It never entered my head that Gaston would fall for you. I was a fool—I knew how Elise had frozen him out of her life, and I should have guessed that when those warm green eyes smiled at him, he would go overboard in five minutes ... you'd had the same effect on me at first sight.' He looked at her hotly. 'You have such a lovely smile, my darling.' A sigh wrenched him. 'You lost it after your fall in the donjon. That hurt more than anything. I felt I had to see you smile again whatever the cost to myself.'

'So you decided to let Hal or Gaston have me?' she asked drily, angry with him for being prepared to let her go if he really loved her.

'I felt I had to let you choose,' he said, almost humbly. 'I can't pretend I found it easy. I was savagely jealous of Gaston when he managed to make contact with you in the hospital after I'd completely failed. You seemed so white and distant whenever I was around, but you broke out of it for Gaston, and I hated him for it. That was why I made sure he went to England; I wanted him out of my hair. Then I thought about it, and I told myself I had to set you free. It hurt like hell, but my conscience made me go on.'

Alex studied his taut, white face carefully. 'And if I had chosen Gaston?'

The flash of the grey eyes was savage. 'I'd have killed

you,' he said, then his mouth twisted. 'No, I'd have made myself bear it. I love you, *mignonne*. I didn't know quite how much until you were almost killed. I almost died myself waiting outside the operating theatre. I knew you had been carrying my child, that it was lost ... but I could bear that. I could not bear to lose you too.'

She put a hand to his hard cheek, turning it towards her, her fingers shaping his face. 'Why did you ignore my invitation after Marie's dinner party? You saw that I wanted you.'

'You were drunk, my darling,' he said grimly. 'I was tempted, believe me, but I'd made up my mind by then to set you free, and I had to walk away. I thought it was just the wine talking.'

She lowered her lashes, her eyes bright. 'Yet now you won't let me go?'

He took her face between his hands, the grey eyes possessive. 'I can't,' he said thickly. 'If you had preferred Hal or Gaston, I would have made myself bear it, but you've turned them both down. I can't just let you walk out of my life, Alex. Let me look after you.' His voice pleaded openly, astonishing her.

Alex looked at him through her long lashes. 'I never expected to hear the dark master of Sarconne beg for anything,' she said softly.

A flush grew on his hard face and his mouth twisted. 'Are you telling me I have to beg, Alex?'

'Would you?' she asked, controlling the shiver in her voice.

He stared at her. 'If I have to,' he muttered, his tone angry.

Her lashes lifted. The green eyes shone towards him, happiness filling them. 'And then you would be violently angry, Monsieur le Comte,' she mocked lovingly. 'Because that pride of yours could never take such a blow.'

He caught the new note in her voice and his hands tightened on her face in a demanding spasm. 'Darling,' he said huskily, 'I'll teach you to love me. You're half-way there already. No woman could have responded as you always did if she felt nothing. We always had that line of communication open, didn't we? This time we'll make it. I should have been honest with you from the start. Only my pride stood in the way, but that died a rapid death when you fell down the donjon steps.'

Her green eyes smiled at him. 'Did it, Philippe?'

His face grew suddenly pale. 'Darling,' he said deeply, 'I've never said ... told you ... how much I wanted the baby, how much it hurt when I knew. I couldn't bear even to speak of it to you. The thought that my child was inside you and ...' His voice broke off with a smothered curse, his eyes tormented.

'Don't, Philippe,' she whispered, pulling one of his hands across her mouth and kissing the palm adoringly. 'There'll be other babies.'

His breath caught. 'Alex,' he groaned, bending his head. The hard, hungry mouth came down and her lips parted eagerly beneath it. She flung her arms round his neck and clung, trembling. Against the pressure of his mouth she whispered, 'Philippe, *je t'aime* ...'

He pushed her head back, staring down into the bright green eyes, an eager, demanding question in his own glance.

'Are you sure?' he asked huskily.

'For a long time I've been certain,' she admitted. 'I don't know when it happened, but I know I love you deeply, Philippe.'

He buried his face in her neck, trembling. 'Come home to Sarconne,' he said. 'I only made this trip to clear things up between us. I couldn't go on without you any longer. If you were going to leave me I preferred to face it right away. Now all I want to do is get you home and start again.'

Her hands stroked his dark hair adoringly. 'Love me,' she whispered. 'Love me now, my darling.'

Eighteen months later, Alex stood in the great hall at Sarconne watching happily as Gisèle, slender and radiant in a full-skirted white wedding dress, revolved around the room in her new husband's arms. After a long and stormy courtship Gisèle had finally given in to the elder son of one of the tenant farmers, a tall, rangy boy with spiky black hair and a tenacious face. They were to set up home in a cottage on the estates, and Philippe thoroughly approved of the match.

It made a cheerful scene. Everyone on the Sarconne estates was present. The wine was flowing like water, Sarconne wine, much appreciated by local people. Philippe had ordered cases of the best vintages to be brought out for Gisèle's wedding, which was doubling as a celebration of the birth of Alex's month-old son, Raoul, who lay now in his cradle in the nursery upstairs, watched over by one of the maids. Lélie's attention had been so centred on the new baby that she had had no time to protest about Gisèle's wedding, despite her view that her daughter was too young to settle down yet. Alex had helped to persuade her to give her permission. Now Lélie laughed as she danced around the room among the other guests, flushed with the new happiness which held Sarconne these days.

Remembering how she had come to the chateau, Alex glowed with satisfaction. She had felt such alarm and misery in those early days. Now she was only aware of happiness, and her happiness had spread across the whole estate. Having a happy family at the chateau had changed everything, like sunshine spreading over a dark landscape.

Philippe joined her, his arm sliding around her waist, and she leaned against him casually, smiling up into his dark, passionate face. 'Gisèle looks rapturously happy,' she said. 'So does Roger.'

'So he should!' Philippe grinned. 'He had quite a battle of it. Who would have thought that our sweet little Gisèle could make such a running fight of her romance?'

'Some women like to be pursued,' she told him, tongue in cheek, her eyes teasing him. 'They enjoy the hunt as much as the hunter does!'

'Do they, indeed?' he asked, his grey eyes flicking from her hair to her warm, smiling mouth. 'You led me a pretty dance, my darling—you should know. But I've got you now and I've no intention of ever letting you go.'

'You ruthless man,' she smiled, green eyes glinting. 'I'm quite sorry for myself. I never had a chance.'

'Not a chance,' he agreed mockingly. 'One look and I knew I was going to have you.'

'The medieval warlord in full pursuit,' she murmured, her mouth laughing.

'Sarconne never gives up its captives,' he told her.

'Never?' She leaned against his arm, pleasurably aware of his strength.

'Never while I have breath, my darling,' he said in

sudden seriousness. He tightened his grip on her, his eyes hungry.

'*Je t'aime,*' she whispered, and the dark master of Sarconne bent to kiss her passionately.

JOY
ROMANCE
LOVE

Harlequin Omnibus
THREE love stories in ONE beautiful volume

The joys of being in love...
the wonder of romance...
the happiness that true love brings ...

Put more love into your life. Experience the wonderful world of...

Harlequin **Romances**

Six brand-new romantic novels every month, each one a thrilling adventure into romance...an exciting glimpse of exotic lands.

Written by world-famous authors, these novels put at your fingertips a fascinating journey into the magic of love, the glamour of faraway places.

Don't wait any longer. Buy them now.